THE COLLECTED WORKS OF BERNARD MALAMUD

REMBRANDT'S HAT

THE COLLECTED WORKS OF BERNARD MALAMUD

REMBRANDT'S HAT

BERNARD MALAMUD

1982

CHATTO & WINDUS

LONDON

37911

Published by
Chatto & Windus Ltd
40 William IV Street
London WC2N 4DF

Of these stories, all slightly revised,
'*Man in the Drawer*', '*Talking Horse*' and
'*In Retirement*' appeared originally in *The Atlantic*.
'*My Son the Murderer*' and '*The Letter*'
appeared originally in *Esquire*.
'*Notes from a Lady at a Dinner Party*'
appeared originally in *Harper's Magazine*.
'*Rembrandt's Hat*' appeared originally in *The New Yorker*.
'*The Silver Crown*' appeared originally in *Playboy*.

British Library Cataloguing in Publication Data
Malamud, Bernard
Rembrandt's hat.—(The collected works
of Bernard Malamud)
I. Title
813'.54[F]   PS3563.A4
ISBN 0–7011–2450–4

Printed in Great Britain by
Redwood Burn Ltd
Trowbridge, Wiltshire

To Ebba, Herb, Hans, George;

and to the memory of Gene

Contents

———

And an old white horse galloped away

in the meadow

T. S. ELIOT

What we want is short cheerful stories

JAMES T. FIELDS *(to Henry James)*

The Silver Crown

G A N S , the father, lay dying in a hospital bed. Different doctors said different things, held different theories. There was talk of an exploratory operation but they thought it might kill him. One doctor said cancer.

"Of the heart," the old man said bitterly.

"It wouldn't be impossible."

The young Gans, Albert, a high school biology teacher, in the afternoons walked the streets in sorrow. What can anybody do about cancer? His soles wore thin with walking. He was easily irritated; angered by the war, atom bomb, pollution, death, obviously the strain of worrying about his father's illness. To be able to do nothing for him made him frantic. He had done nothing for him all his life.

A female colleague, an English teacher he had slept with once, a girl who was visibly aging, advised, "If the doctors don't know, Albert, try a faith healer. Different people know different things; nobody knows everything. You can't tell about the human body."

Albert laughed mirthlessly but listened. If specialists disagree who do you agree with? If you've tried everything what else can you try?

One afternoon after a long walk alone, as he was about to descend the subway stairs somewhere in the Bronx, still burdened by his worries, uneasy that nothing had changed, he was accosted by a fat girl with bare meaty arms who thrust a soiled card at him that he tried to avoid. She was a stupefying sight, retarded at the very least. Fifteen, he'd say, though she looks thirty and probably has the mentality of age ten. Her skin glowed, face wet, fleshy, the small mouth open and would be forever; eyes set wide apart on the broad unfocused face, either washed-out green or brown, or one of each—he wasn't sure. She seemed not to mind his appraisal, gurgled faintly. Her thick hair was braided in two ropelike strands; she wore bulging cloth slippers, bursting at seams and soles; a faded red skirt down to massive ankles; and a heavy brown sweater vest, buttoned over blown breasts, though the weather was still hot September.

The teacher's impulse was to pass by her outthrust plump baby hand. Instead he took the card from her. Simple curiosity—once you had learned to read you read anything? Charitable impulse?

Albert recognized Yiddish and Hebrew but read in English: "Heal The Sick. Save The Dying. Make A Silver Crown."

"What kind of silver crown would that be?"

She uttered impossible noises. Depressed, he looked away. When his eyes turned to hers she ran off.

He studied the card. "Make A Silver Crown." It gave a rabbi's name and address no less: Jonas Lifschitz, close by in the neighborhood. The silver crown mystified him. He had no idea what it had to do with saving the dying but felt he ought to know. Although at first repelled by the thought, he made up his mind to visit the rabbi and felt, in a way, relieved.

The teacher hastened along the street a few blocks until he came to the address on the card, a battered synagogue in a store, Congregation Theodor Herzl, painted in large uneven white letters on the plate-glass window. The rabbi's name, in smaller, gold letters, was A. Marcus. In the doorway to the left of the store the number of the house was repeated in tin numerals, and on a card under the vacant name plate under the mezuzah, appeared in pencil, "Rabbi J. Lifschitz. Retired. Consultations. Ring The Bell." The bell, when he decided to chance it, did not work— seemed dead to the touch—so Albert, his heartbeat erratic, turned the knob. The door gave easily enough and he hesitantly walked up a dark flight of narrow wooden stairs.

Ascending, assailed by doubts, peering up through the gloom, he thought of turning back but at the first-floor landing compelled himself to knock loudly on the door.

"Anybody home here?"

He rapped harder, annoyed with himself for being there, engaging in the act of entrance—who would have predicted it an hour ago? The door opened a crack and that broad, badly formed face appeared. The retarded girl, squinting one bulbous eye, made noises like two eggs frying, and ducked back, slamming the door. The teacher, after momentary reflection, thrust it open in time to see her, bulky as she was, running swiftly along the long tight corridor, her body bumping the walls before she disappeared into a room at the rear.

Albert entered cautiously, with a sense of embarrassment, if not danger, warning himself to depart at once; yet stayed to peek curiously into a front room off the hallway, darkened by lowered green shades through which thread-like rivulets of light streamed. The shades resembled faded maps of ancient lands. An old gray-bearded man with thickened left eyelid, wearing a yarmulke, sat heavily asleep, a book in his lap, on a sagging armchair. Someone in the room gave off a stale odor, unless it was the armchair. As Albert stared, the old man awoke in a hurry. The small thick book on his lap fell with a thump to the floor, but instead of picking it up, he shoved it with a kick of his heel under the chair.

"So where were we?" he inquired pleasantly, a bit breathless.

The teacher removed his hat, remembered whose house he was in, and put it back on his head.

He introduced himself. "I was looking for Rabbi J. Lifschitz. Your—ah—girl let me in."

"Rabbi Lifschitz; this was my daughter Rifkele. She's not perfect, though God who made her in His image is Himself perfection. What this means I don't have to tell you."

His heavy eyelid went down in a wink, apparently involuntarily.

"What does it mean?" Albert asked.

"In her way she is also perfect."

"Anyway she let me in and here I am."

"So what did you decide?"

"Concerning what if I may ask?"

"What did you decide about what we were talking about—the silver crown?"

His eyes roved as he spoke; he rubbed a nervous thumb and forefinger. Crafty type, the teacher decided. Him I have to watch myself with.

"I came here to find out about this crown you advertised," he said, "but actually we haven't talked about it or anything else. When I entered here you were sound asleep."

"At my age—" the rabbi explained with a little laugh.

"I don't mean any criticism. All I'm saying is I am a stranger to you."

"How can we be strangers if we both believe in God?"

Albert made no argument of it.

The rabbi raised the two shades and the last of day-light fell into the spacious high-ceilinged room, crowded with at least a dozen stiff-back and folding chairs, plus a broken sofa. What kind of operation is he running here? Group consultations? He dispensed rabbinic therapy? The teacher felt renewed distaste for himself for having come. On the wall hung a single oval mirror, framed in gold-plated groupings of joined metal circles, large and small; but no pictures. Despite the empty chairs, or perhaps because of them, the room seemed barren.

The teacher observed that the rabbi's trousers were a week from ragged. He was wearing an unpressed worn black suit-coat and a yellowed white shirt without a tie. His wet grayish-blue eyes were restless. Rabbi Lifschitz was a dark-faced man with brown eye pouches and smelled of old age. This was the odor. It was hard to say whether he resembled his daughter; Rifkele resembled her species.

"So sit," said the old rabbi with a light sigh. "Not on the couch, sit on a chair."

"Which in particular?"

"You have a first-class humor." Smiling absently he pointed to two kitchen chairs and seated himself in one.

He offered a thin cigarette.

"I'm off them," the teacher explained.

"I also." The old man put the pack away. "So who is sick?" he inquired.

Albert tightened at the question as he recalled the card he had taken from the girl: "Heal The Sick, Save The Dying."

"To come to the point, my father's in the hospital with a serious ailment. In fact he's dying."

The rabbi, nodding gravely, dug into his pants pocket for a pair of glasses, wiped them with a large soiled handkerchief and put them on, lifting the wire earpieces over each fleshy ear.

"So we will make then a crown for him?"

"That depends. The crown is what I came here to find out about."

"What do you wish to find out?"

"I'll be frank with you." The teacher blew his nose and slowly wiped it. "My cast of mind is naturally empiric and objective—you might say non-mystical. I'm suspicious of faith healing but I've come here, frankly, because I want to do anything possible to help my father recover his former health. To put it otherwise, I don't want anything to go untried."

"You love your father?" the rabbi clucked, a glaze of sentiment veiling his eyes.

"What I feel is obvious. My real concern right now mainly is how does the crown work. Could you be explicit about the mechanism of it all? Who wears it, for instance? Does he? Do you? Or do I have to? In other words, how does it function? And if you wouldn't mind saying, what's the principle, or rationale, behind it? This is terra incognita for me, but I think I might be willing to take a chance if I could justify it to myself. Could I see a sample of the crown, for instance, if you have one on hand?"

The rabbi, with an absent-minded start, seemed to interrupt himself about to pick his nose.

"What is the crown?" he asked, at first haughtily, then again, gently. "It's a crown, nothing else. There are crowns in Mishna, Proverbs, Kabbalah; the holy scrolls of the Torah are often protected by crowns. But this one is different, this you will understand when it does the work. It's a miracle. A sample doesn't exist. The crown has to be made individual for your father. Then his health will be restored. There are two prices—"

"Kindly explain what's supposed to cure the sickness," Albert said. "Does it work like sympathetic magic? I'm not nay-saying, you understand. I just happen to be interested in all kinds of phenomena. Is the crown supposed to draw off the illness like some kind of poultice, or what?"

"The crown is not a medicine, it is the health of your father. We offer the crown to God and God returns to your father his health. But first we got to make it the way it must be made—this I will do with my assistant, a retired jeweler. He has helped me to make a thousand crowns. Believe me, he knows silver—the right amount to the ounce according to the size you wish. Then I will say the blessings. Without the right blessings, exact to each word, the crown don't work. I don't have to tell you why. When the crown is finished your father will get better. This I will guarantee you. Let me read you some words from the mystic book."

"The Kabbalah?" the teacher asked respectfully.

"Like the Kabbalah."

The rabbi rose, went to his armchair, got slowly down on his hands and knees and withdrew the book he had shoved under the misshapen chair, a thick small volume with faded purple covers, not a word imprinted on it. The rabbi kissed the book and murmured a prayer.

"I hid it for a minute," he explained, "when you came in the room. It's a terrible thing nowadays, goyim come in your house in the middle of the day and take away that which belongs to you, if not your life itself."

"I told you right away that your daughter had let me in," Albert said in embarrassment.

"Once you mentioned I knew."

The teacher then asked, "Suppose I am a non-believer? Will the crown work if it's ordered by a person who has his doubts?"

"Doubts we all got. We doubt God and God doubts us. This is natural on account of the nature of existence. Of this kind doubts I am not afraid so long as you love your father."

"You're putting it as sort of a paradox."

"So what's so bad about a paradox?"

"My father wasn't the easiest man in the world to get along with, and neither am I for that matter, but he has been generous to me and I'd like to repay him in some way."

"God respects a grateful son. If you love your father this will go in the crown and help him to recover his health. Do you understand Hebrew?"

"Unfortunately not."

The rabbi flipped a few pages of his thick tome, peered at one closely and read aloud in Hebrew which he then translated into English. " 'The crown is the fruit of God's grace. His grace is love of creation.' These words I will read seven times over the silver crown. This is the most important blessing."

"Fine. But what about those two prices you mentioned a minute ago?"

"This depends how quick you wish the cure."

"I want the cure to be immediate, otherwise there's no sense to the whole deal," Albert said, controlling anger. "If you're questioning my sincerity, I've already told you I'm considering this recourse even though it goes against the grain of some of my strongest convictions. I've gone out of my way to make my pros and cons absolutely clear."

"Who says no?"

The teacher became aware of Rifkele standing at the door, eating a slice of bread with lumps of butter on it. She beheld him in mild stupefaction, as though seeing him for the first time.

"Shpeter, Rifkele," the rabbi said patiently.

The girl shoved the bread into her mouth and ran ponderously down the passageway.

"Anyway, what about those two prices?" Albert asked, annoyed by the interruption. Every time Rifkele appeared his doubts of the enterprise rose before him like warriors with spears.

"We got two kinds crowns," said the rabbi. "One is for 401 and the other is 986."

"Dollars, you mean, for God's sake?—that's fantastic."

"The crown is pure silver. The client pays in silver

dollars. So the silver dollars we melt—more for the large-size crown, less for the medium."

"What about the small?"

"There is no small. What good is a small crown?"

"I wouldn't know, but the assumption seems to be the bigger the better. Tell me, please, what can a 986 crown do that a 401 can't? Does the patient get better faster with the larger one? It hastens the reaction?"

The rabbi, five fingers hidden in his limp beard, assented.

"Are there any other costs?"

"Costs?"

"Over and above the quoted prices?"

"The price is the price, there is no extra. The price is for the silver and for the work and for the blessings."

"Now would you kindly tell me, assuming I decide to get involved in this, where am I supposed to lay my hands on 401 silver dollars? Or if I should opt for the 986 job, where can I get a pile of cartwheels of that amount? I don't suppose that any bank in the whole Bronx would keep that many silver dollars on hand nowadays. The Bronx is no longer the Wild West, Rabbi Lifschitz. But what's more to the point, isn't it true the mint isn't making silver dollars all silver any more?"

"So if they are not making we will get wholesale. If you will leave with me the cash I will order the silver from a wholesaler, and we will save you the trouble to go to the bank. It will be the same amount of silver, only in small bars, I will weigh them on a scale in front of your eyes."

"One other question. Would you take my personal check in payment? I could give it to you right away once I've made my final decision."

"I wish I could, Mr. Gans," said the rabbi, his veined hand still nervously exploring his beard, "but it's better cash when the patient is so sick, so I can start to work right away. A check sometimes comes back, or gets lost in the bank, and this interferes with the crown."

Albert did not ask how, suspecting that a bounced check, or a lost one, wasn't the problem. No doubt some customers for crowns had stopped their checks on afterthought.

As the teacher reflected concerning his next move—should he, shouldn't he?—weighing a rational thought against a sentimental, the old rabbi sat in his chair, reading quickly in his small mystic book, his lips hastening along silently.

Albert at last got up.

"I'll decide the question once and for all tonight. If I go ahead and commit myself on the crown I'll bring you the cash after work tomorrow."

"Go in good health," said the rabbi. Removing his glasses he wiped both eyes with his handkerchief.

Wet or dry? thought the teacher.

As he let himself out of the downstairs door, more inclined than not toward trying the crown, he felt relieved, almost euphoric.

But by the next morning, after a difficult night, Albert's mood had about-faced. He fought gloom, irritation, felt flashes of hot and cold anger. It's throwing money away, pure and simple. I'm dealing with a clever confidence man, that's plain to me, but for some reason I am not resisting strongly. Maybe my subconscious is telling me to go along with a blowing wind and have the crown made. After that we'll see what happens—whether it rains, snows, or spring comes. Not much will happen, I suppose, but whatever does, my conscience will be in the clear.

But when he visited Rabbi Lifschitz that afternoon in the same roomful of empty chairs, though the teacher carried the required cash in his wallet, he was still uncomfortable about parting with it.

"Where do the crowns go after they are used and the patient recovers his health?" he cleverly asked the rabbi.

"I'm glad you asked me this question," said the rabbi alertly, his thick lid drooping. "They are melted and the silver we give to the poor. A mitzvah for one makes a mitzvah for another."

"To the poor you say?"

"There are plenty poor people, Mr. Gans. Sometimes they need a crown for a sick wife or a sick child. Where will they get the silver?"

"I see what you mean—recycled, sort of, but can't a crown be re-used as it is? I mean do you permit a period of time to go by before you melt them down? Suppose a dying man who recovers gets seriously ill again at a future date?"

"For a new sickness you will need a new crown. Tomorrow the world is not the same as today, though God listens with the same ear."

"Look, Rabbi Lifschitz," Albert said impatiently, "I'll tell you frankly that I am inching toward ordering the crown, but it would make my decision a whole lot easier all around if you would let me have a quick look at one of them—it wouldn't have to be for more than five seconds—at a crown-in-progress for some other client."

"What will you see in five seconds?"

"Enough—whether the object is believable, worth the fuss and not inconsequential investment."

"Mr. Gans," replied the rabbi, "this is not a showcase business. You are not buying from me a new Chevrolet automobile. Your father lays now dying in the hospital. Do you love him? Do you wish me to make a crown that will cure him?"

The teacher's anger flared. "Don't be stupid, rabbi, I've answered that. Please don't sidetrack the real issue. You're working on my guilt so I'll suspend my perfectly reasonable doubts of the whole freaking business. I won't fall for that."

They glared at each other. The rabbi's beard quivered. Albert ground his teeth.

Rifkele, in a nearby room, moaned.

The rabbi, breathing emotionally, after a moment relented.

"I will show you the crown," he sighed.

"Accept my apologies for losing my temper."

The rabbi accepted. "Now tell me please what kind of sickness your father has got."

"Ah," said Albert, "nobody is certain for sure. One day

he got into bed, turned to the wall and said, 'I'm sick.' They suspected leukemia at first but the lab tests didn't confirm it."

"You talked to the doctors?"

"In droves. Till I was blue in the face. A bunch of ignoramuses," said the teacher hoarsely. "Anyway, nobody knows exactly what he has wrong with him. The theories include rare blood diseases, also a possible carcinoma of certain endocrine glands. You name it, I've heard it, with complications suggested, like Parkinson's or Addison's disease, multiple sclerosis, or something similar, alone or in combination with other sicknesses. It's a mysterious case, all in all."

"This means you will need a special crown," said the rabbi.

The teacher bridled. "What do you mean special? What will it cost?"

"The cost will be the same," the rabbi answered dryly, "but the design and the kind of blessings will be different. When you are dealing with such a mystery you got to make another one but it must be bigger."

"How would that work?"

"Like two winds that they meet in the sky. A white and a blue. The blue says, 'Not only I am blue but inside I am also purple and orange.' So the white goes away."

"If you can work it up for the same price, that's up to you."

Rabbi Lifschitz then drew down the two green window shades and shut the door, darkening the room.

"Sit," he said in the heavy dark, "I will show you the crown."

"I'm sitting."

"So sit where you are, but turn your head to the wall where is the mirror."

"But why so dark?"

"You will see light."

He heard the rabbi strike a match and it flared momentarily, casting shadows of candles and chairs amid the empty chairs in the room.

"Look now in the mirror."

"I'm looking."

"What do you see?"

"Nothing."

"Look with your eyes."

A silver candelabrum, first with three, then five, then seven burning bony candlesticks appeared like ghostly hands with flaming fingertips in the oval mirror. The heat of it hit Albert in the face and for a moment he was stunned.

But recalling the games of his childhood, he thought, who's kidding who? It's one of those illusion things I remember from when I was a kid. In that case I'm getting the hell out of here. I can stand maybe mystery but not magic tricks or dealing with a rabbinical magician.

The candelabrum had vanished, although not its light, and he now saw the rabbi's somber face in the glass, his gaze addressing him. Albert glanced quickly around to see if anyone was standing at his shoulder, but nobody was. Where the rabbi was hiding at the moment the teacher did not know; but in the lit glass appeared his old man's lined and shrunken face, his sad eyes, compelling, inquisitive, weary, perhaps even frightened, as though they had seen more than they had cared to but were still looking.

What's this, slides or home movies? Albert sought some source of projection but saw no ray of light from wall or ceiling, nor object or image that might be reflected by the mirror.

The rabbi's eyes glowed like sun-filled clouds. A moon rose in the blue sky. The teacher dared not move, afraid to discover he was unable to. He then beheld a shining crown on the rabbi's head.

It had appeared at first like a braided mother-of-pearl turban, then had luminously become—like an intricate star in the night sky—a silver crown, constructed of bars, triangles, half-moons and crescents, spires, turrets, trees, points of spears; as though a wild storm had swept them up from the earth and flung them together in its vortex, twisted into a single glowing interlocked sculpture, a forest of disparate objects.

The sight in the ghostly mirror, a crown of rare beauty —very impressive, Albert thought—lasted no longer than five short seconds, then the reflecting glass by degrees turned dark and empty.

The shades were up. The single bulb in a frosted lily fixture on the ceiling shone harshly in the room. It was night.

The old rabbi sat, exhausted, on the broken sofa.

"So you saw it?"

"I saw something."

"You believe what you saw—the crown?"

"I believe I saw. Anyway, I'll take it."

The rabbi gazed at him blankly.

"I mean I agree to have the crown made," Albert said, having to clear his throat.

"Which size?"

"Which size was the one I saw?"

"Both sizes. This is the same design for both sizes, but there is more silver and also more blessings for the $986 size."

"But didn't you say that the design for my father's crown, because of the special nature of his illness, would have a different style, plus some special blessings?"

The rabbi nodded. "This comes also in two sizes—the $401 and $986."

The teacher hesitated a split second. "Make it the big one," he said decisively.

He had his wallet in his hand and counted out fifteen new bills—nine one hundreds, four twenties, a five and a single—adding to $986.

Putting on his glasses, the rabbi hastily counted the money, snapping with thumb and forefinger each crisp bill as though to be sure none had stuck together. He folded the stiff paper and thrust the wad into his pants pocket.

"Could I have a receipt?"

"I would like to give you a receipt," said Rabbi Lifschitz earnestly, "but for the crowns there are no receipts. Some things are not a business."

"If money is exchanged, why not?"

"God will not allow. My father did not give receipts and also my grandfather."

"How can I prove I paid you if something goes wrong?"

"You have my word, nothing will go wrong."

"Yes, but suppose something unforeseen did," Albert insisted, "would you return the cash?"

"Here is your cash," said the rabbi, handing the teacher the packet of folded bills.

"Never mind," said Albert hastily. "Could you tell me when the crown will be ready?"

"Tomorrow night before Shabbos, the latest."

"So soon?"

"Your father is dying."

"That's right, but the crown looks like a pretty intricate piece of work to put together out of all those odd pieces."

"We will hurry."

"I wouldn't want you to rush the job in any way that would—let's say—prejudice the potency of the crown, or for that matter, in any way impair the quality of it as I saw it in the mirror—or however I saw it."

Down came the rabbi's eyelid, quickly raised without a sign of self-consciousness.

"Mr. Gans, all my crowns are first-class jobs. About this you got nothing to worry about."

They then shook hands. Albert, still assailed by doubts, stepped into the corridor. He felt he did not, in essence, trust the rabbi; and suspected that Rabbi Lifschitz knew it and did not, in essence, trust him.

Rifkele, panting like a cow for a bull, let him out the front door, perfectly.

In the subway, Albert figured he would call it an investment in experience and see what came of it. Education costs money but how else can you get it? He pictured the crown as he had seen it established on the rabbi's head, and then seemed to remember that as he had stared at the man's shifty face in the mirror the thickened lid of his right eye had slowly dropped into a full wink. Did he recall this in truth, or was he seeing in his mind's eye and transposing into the past something that had happened just before he left the house? What does he mean by his wink?— not only is he a fake but he kids you? Uneasy once more, the teacher clearly remembered, when he was staring into the rabbi's fish eyes in the glass, after which they had lit in visionary light, that he had fought a hunger to sleep; and the next thing there's the sight of the old boy, as though on the television screen, wearing this high-hat magic crown.

Albert, rising, cried, "Hypnosis! The bastard magician hypnotized me! He never did produce a silver crown, it's out of my imagination—I've been suckered!"

He was outraged by the knavery, hypocrisy, fat nerve of Rabbi Jonas Lifschitz. The concept of a curative crown, if he had ever for a moment believed in it, crumbled in his brain and all he could think of were 986 blackbirds flying in the sky. As three curious passengers watched, Albert bolted out of the car at the next stop, rushed up the stairs, hurried across the street, then cooled his impatient heels for twenty-two minutes till the next train clattered into the station, and he rode back to the stop near the rabbi's house. Though he banged with both fists on the door, kicked at it, "rang" the useless bell until his thumb was blistered, the boxlike wooden house, including dilapidated synagogue store, was dark, monumentally starkly still, like a gigantic, slightly tilted tombstone in a vast graveyard; and in the end unable to arouse a soul, the teacher, long past midnight, had to head home.

He awoke next morning cursing the rabbi and his own stupidity for having got involved with a faith healer. This is what happens when a man—even for a minute—surrenders his true beliefs. There are less punishing ways to help the dying. Albert considered calling the cops but had no receipt and did not want to appear that much a fool. He was tempted, for the first time in six years of teaching, to phone in sick; then take a cab to the rabbi's house and demand the return of his cash. The thought agitated him. On the other hand, suppose Rabbi Lifschitz was seriously at work assembling the crown with his helper; on which, let's say, after he had bought the silver and paid the retired jeweler for his work, he made, let's say, a hundred bucks clear profit—not so very much; and there really *was* a silver crown, and the rabbi sincerely and religiously believed it would reverse the course of his father's illness? Although nervously disturbed by his suspicions, Albert felt he had better not get the police into the act too soon because the crown wasn't promised—didn't the old gent say—until before the Sabbath, which gave him till sunset tonight.

If he produces the thing by then, I have no case against him even if it's a piece of junk. So I better wait. But what a dope I was to order the $986 job instead of the $401. On that decision alone I lost $585.

After a distracted day's work Albert taxied to the rabbi's house and tried to rouse him, even hallooing at the blank windows facing the street; but either nobody was home or they were both hiding, the rabbi under the broken sofa, Rifkele trying to shove her bulk under a bathtub. Albert decided to wait them out. Soon the old boy would have to leave the house to step into the shul on Friday night. He would speak to him, warn him to come clean. But the sun set; dusk settled on the earth; and though the autumn stars and a sliver of moon gleamed in the sky, the house was dark, shades drawn; and no Rabbi Lifschitz emerged. Lights had gone on in the little shul, candles were lit. It occurred to Albert, with chagrin, that the rabbi might be already worshipping; he might all this time have been in the synagogue.

The teacher entered the long, brightly lit store. On yellow folding chairs scattered around the room sat a dozen men holding worn prayer books, praying. The Rabbi A. Marcus, a middle-aged man with a high voice and a short reddish beard, was dovening at the Ark, his back to the congregation.

As Albert entered and embarrassedly searched from face to face, the congregants stared at him. The old rabbi was not among them. Disappointed, the teacher withdrew.

A man sitting by the door touched his sleeve.

"Stay awhile and read with us."

"Excuse me, I'd like to but I'm looking for a friend."

"Look," said the man, "maybe you'll find him."

Albert waited across the street under a chestnut tree losing its leaves. He waited patiently—till tomorrow if he had to.

Shortly after nine the lights went out in the synagogue and the last of the worshippers left for home. The red-bearded rabbi then emerged with his key in his hand to lock the store door.

"Excuse me, rabbi," said Albert, approaching. "Are you acquainted with Rabbi Jonas Lifschitz, who lives upstairs with his daughter Rifkele—if she is his daughter?"

"He used to come here," said the rabbi with a small smile, "but since he retired he prefers a big synagogue on Mosholu Parkway, a palace."

"Will he be home soon, do you think?"

"Maybe in an hour. It's Shabbat, he must walk."

"Do you—ah—happen to know anything about his work on silver crowns?"

"What kind of silver crowns?"

"To assist the sick, the dying?"

"No," said the rabbi, locking the shul door, pocketing the key, and hurrying away.

The teacher, eating his heart, waited under the chestnut tree till past midnight, all the while urging himself to give up and go home but unable to unstick the glue of his frustration and rage. Then shortly before 1 a.m. he saw some shadows moving and two people drifting up the shadow-encrusted street. One was the old rabbi, in a new caftan and snappy black Homburg, walking tiredly. Rifkele, in sexy yellow mini, exposing to above the big-bone knees her legs like poles, walked lightly behind him, stopping to strike her ears with her hands. A long white shawl, pulled short on the right shoulder, hung down to her left shoe.

"On my income their glad rags."

Rifkele chanted a long "boooo" and slapped both ears with her pudgy hands to keep from hearing it.

They toiled up the ill-lit narrow staircase, the teacher trailing them.

"I came to see my crown," he told the pale, astonished rabbi, in the front room.

"The crown," the rabbi said haughtily, "is already finished. Go home and wait, your father will soon get better."

"I called the hospital before leaving my apartment, there's been no improvement."

"How can you expect so soon improvement if the doctors themselves don't know what is the sickness? You must give the crown a little more time. God Himself has trouble to understand human sickness."

"I came to see the thing I paid for."

"I showed you already, you saw before you ordered."

"That was an image of a facsimile, maybe, or something of the sort. I insist on seeing the real thing, for which I paid close to one thousand smackers."

"Listen, Mr. Gans," said the rabbi patiently, "there are some things we are allowed to see which He lets us see them. Sometimes I wish He didn't let us. There are other things we are not allowed to see—Moses knew this—and one is God's face, and another is the real crown that He makes and blesses it. A miracle is a miracle, this is God's business."

"Don't you see it?"

"Not with my eyes."

"I don't believe a word of it, you faker, two-bit magician."

"The crown is a real crown. If you think there is magic, it is on account those people that they insist to see it—we try to give them an idea. For those who believe, there is no magic."

"Rifkele," the rabbi said hurriedly, "bring to Papa my book of letters."

She left the room, after a while, a little in fright, her eyes evasive; and returned in ten minutes, after flushing the toilet, in a shapeless long flannel nightgown, carrying a large yellowed notebook whose loose pages were thickly interleaved with old correspondence.

"Testimonials," said the rabbi.

Turning several loose pages, with trembling hand he extracted a letter and read it aloud, his voice husky with emotion.

" 'Dear Rabbi Lifschitz: Since the miraculous recovery of my mother, Mrs. Max Cohen, from her recent illness, my impulse is to cover your bare feet with kisses. Your crown worked wonders and I am recommending it to all my friends. Yours truly and sincerely, (Mrs.) Esther Polatnik.' "

"This is a college teacher."

He read another. " 'Dear Rabbi Lifschitz, Your $986 crown totally and completely cured my father of cancer of the pancreas, with serious complications of the lungs, after nothing else had worked. Never before have I believed in miraculous occurrences, but from now on I will have less doubts. My thanks to you and God. Most sincerely, Daniel Schwartz.' "

"A lawyer," said the rabbi.

He offered the book to Albert. "Look yourself, Mr. Gans, hundreds of letters."

Albert wouldn't touch it.

"There's only one thing I want to look at, Rabbi Lifschitz, and it's not a book of useless testimonials. I want to see my father's silver crown."

"This is impossible. I already explained to you why I can't do this. God's word is God's law."

"So if it's the law you're citing, either I see the crown in the next five minutes, or the first thing tomorrow morning I'm reporting you and your activities to the Bronx County District Attorney."

"Booo-ooo," sang Rifkele, banging her ears.

"Shut up!" Albert said.

"Have respect," cried the rabbi. "Grubber yung!"

"I will swear out a complaint and the D.A. will shut

you down, the whole freaking plant, if you don't at once return the $986 you swindled me out of."

The rabbi wavered in his tracks. "Is this the way to talk to a rabbi of God?"

"A thief is a thief."

Rifkele blubbered, squealed.

"Sha," the rabbi thickly whispered to Albert, clasping and unclasping his gray hands. "You'll frighten the neighbors. Listen to me, Mr. Gans, you saw with your eyes what it looks like the real crown. I give you my word that nobody of my whole clientele ever saw this before. I showed you for your father's sake so you would tell me to make the crown which will save him. Don't spoil now the miracle."

"Miracle," Albert bellowed, "it's a freaking fake magic, with an idiot girl for a come-on and hypnotic mirrors. I was mesmerized, suckered by you."

"Be kind," begged the rabbi, tottering as he wandered amid empty chairs. "Be merciful to an old man. Think of my poor child. Think of your father who loves you."

"He hates me, the son-of-a-bitch, I hope he croaks."

In an explosion of silence the girl slobbered in fright.

"Aha," cried the wild-eyed rabbi, pointing a finger at God in heaven.

"Murderer," he cried, aghast.

Moaning, father and daughter rushed into each other's arms, as Albert, wearing a massive, spike-laden headache, rushed down the booming stairs.

An hour later the elder Gans shut his eyes and expired.

Man in the Drawer

—

A SOFT shalom I thought I heard, but considering the Slavic cast of the driver's face, it seemed unlikely. He had been eyeing me in his rear-view mirror since I had stepped into the taxi and, to tell the truth, I had momentary apprehensions. I'm forty-seven and have recently lost weight but not, I confess, nervousness. It's my American clothes, I thought at first. One is a recognizable stranger. Unless he had been tailing me to begin with, but how could that be if it was a passing cab I had hailed myself?

He had picked me up in his noisy Volga of ancient vintage on the Lenin Hills, where I had been wandering all afternoon in and around Moscow University. Finally I'd had enough of sightseeing, and when I saw the cab, hallooed and waved both arms. The driver, cruising in a hurry, had stopped, you might say, on a kopek, as though I were someone he was dying to give a ride to; maybe somebody he had mistaken for a friend. Considering my recent experiences in Kiev, a friend was someone I wouldn't mind being mistaken for.

From the moment we met, our eyes were caught in a developing recognition although we were complete strangers. I knew nobody in Moscow except an Intourist girl or two. In the mottled mirror his face seemed mildly distorted —badly reflected; but not the eyes, small, canny, curious— they probed, tugged, doubted, seemed to beg to know: give him a word and he'd be grateful, though why and for what cause he didn't say. Then, as if the whole thing wearied him insufferably, he pretended no further interest.

Serves him right, I thought, but it wouldn't hurt if he paid a little attention to the road now and then or we'll never get where we're going, wherever that is. I realized I hadn't said because I wasn't sure myself—anywhere but back to the Metropole just yet. It was one of those days I couldn't stand a hotel room.

"Shalom!" he said finally out loud.

"Shalom to you." So it was what I had heard, who would have thought so? We both relaxed, looking at opposite sides of the street.

The taxi driver sat in his shirt sleeves on a cool June day, not more than $55°$ Fahrenheit. He was a man in his thirties who looked as if what he ate didn't fully feed him— in afterthought a discontented type, his face on the tired side; not bad-looking—now that I'd studied him a little, even though the head seemed pressed a bit flat by some- body's heavy hand although protected by a mat of healthy hair. His face, as I said, veered to Slavic: round; broad cheekbones, small firm chin; but he sported also a longish nose and a distinctive larynx on a slender hairy neck; a mixed type, it appeared. At any rate, the shalom had seemed to alter his appearance, even of the probing eyes. He was dissatisfied for certain this fine June day—his job, fate, appearance—what? And a sort of indigenous sadness hung on him, coming God knows from where; nor did he seem to mind if who he was was immediately visible; not everybody could do that or wanted to. This one showed himself. Not too prosperous, I would say, yet no under- ground man. He sat firm in his seat, all of him driving, a touch frantically. I have an experienced eye for such details.

"Israeli?" he asked in a whisper.

"Amerikansky." I know no Russian, just a few polite words.

He dug into his shirt pocket for a thin pack of ciga- rettes and swung his arm over the seat, the Volga swerving to avoid a truck making a turn.

"Take care!"

I was thrown sideways—no apologies. Extracting a Bulgarian cigarette I wasn't eager to smoke—too strong—I handed him his pack. I was considering offering my prosperous American cigarettes in return but didn't want to affront him.

"Feliks Levitansky," he said. "How do you do? I am the taxi driver." His accent was strong, verging on fruity, but redeemed by fluency of tongue.

"Ah, you speak English? I sort of thought so."

"My profession is translator—English, French." He shrugged sideways.

"Howard Harvitz is my name. I'm here for a short vacation, about three weeks. My wife died not so long ago, and I'm traveling partly to relieve my mind."

My voice caught, but then I went on to say that if I could manage to dig up some material for a magazine article or two, so much the better.

In sympathy Levitansky raised both hands from the wheel.

"Watch out, for God's sake!"

"Horovitz?" he asked.

I spelled it for him. "Frankly, it was Harris after I entered college but I changed it back recently. My father had it legally changed after I graduated from high school. He was a doctor, a practical sort."

"You don't look to me Jewish."

"If so why did you say shalom?"

"Sometimes you say." After a minute he asked, "For which reason?"

"For which reason what?"

"Why you changed back your name?"

"I had a crisis in my life."

"Existential? Economic?"

"To tell the truth I changed it back after my wife died."

"What is the significance?"

"The significance is I am closer to my true self."

The driver popped a match with his thumbnail and lit his cigarette.

"I am marginal Jew," he said, "although my father— Avrahm Isaakovich Levitansky—was Jewish. Because my mother was gentile woman I was given choice, but she insisted me to register for internal passport with notation of Jewish nationality in respect for my father. I did so."

"You don't say?"

"My father died in my childhood. I was rised—raised? —to respect Jewish people and religion but I went my own way. I am atheist. This is almost inevitable."

"You mean Soviet life?"

Levitansky smoked without replying as I grew embarrassed by my question. I looked around to see if I knew where we were. In afterthought he asked, "to which destination?"

I said, still on the former subject, that I had been not much of a Jew myself. "My mother and father were totally assimilated."

"By their choice?"

"Of course by their choice."

"Do you wish," he then asked, "to visit Central Synagogue on Arkhipova Street? Very interesting experience."

"Not just now," I said, "but take me to the Chekhov
Museum on Sadovaya Kudrinskaya."

At that the driver, sighing, seemed to take heart.

Rose, I said to myself.

I blew my nose. After her death I had planned to visit
the Soviet Union but couldn't get myself to move. I'm a
slow man after a blow, though I confess I've never been one
for making his mind up in a hurry about important things.
Eight months later, when I was more or less packing, I
felt that some of the relief I was looking for derived, in
addition to what was still on my mind, from the necessity
of making an unexpected serious personal decision. Out of
loneliness I had begun to see my former wife, Lillian, in
the spring; and before long, since she had remained unmar-
ried and still attractive, to my surprise there was some
hesitant talk of remarriage; these things slip from one
sentence to another before you know it. If we did get married we could turn the Russian trip into a sort of honey-
moon—I won't say second because we hadn't had much of
a first. In the end, since our lives had been so frankly
complicated—hard on each other—I found it impossible to
make up my mind, though Lillian, I give her credit,
seemed to be willing to take the chance. My feelings were
so difficult to define to myself I decided to decide nothing
for sure. Lillian, who is a forthright type with a mind like
a lawyer's, asked me if I was cooling off to the idea, and I
told her that since the death of my wife I had been examin-

ing my life and needed more time to see where I stood. "Still?" she said, meaning the self-searching, and implying, I thought, forever. All I could answer was "Still," and then in anger, "Forever." I warned myself afterward: Beware of any more complicated entanglements.

Well, that almost killed it. It wasn't a particularly happy evening, though it had its moments. I had once been very much in love with Lillian. I figured then that a change of scene for me, maybe a month abroad, might be helpful. I had for a long time wanted to visit the U.S.S.R., and taking the time to be alone and, I hoped, at ease to think things through, might give the trip additional value.

So I was surprised, once my visa was granted—though not too surprised—that my anticipation was by now blunted and I was experiencing some uneasiness. I blamed it on a dread of traveling that sometimes hits me before long trips, that I have to make my peace with before I can move. Will I get there? Will the plane be hijacked? Maybe a war breaks out and I'm surrounded by artillery. To be frank, though I've resisted the idea, I consider myself an anxious man, which, when I try to explain it to myself, means being this minute halfway into the next. I sit still in a hurry, worry uselessly about the future, and carry the burden of an overripe conscience.

I realized that what troubled me mostly about going into Soviet Russia were those stories in the papers of some tourist or casual traveler in this or that Soviet city, who is, without warning, grabbed by the secret police on charges of "spying," "illegal economic activity," "hooligan-

ism," or whatnot. This poor guy, like somebody from Sud-
bury, Mass., is held incommunicado until he confesses, and
is then sentenced to a prison camp in the wilds of Siberia.
After I got my visa I sometimes had fantasies of a stranger
shoving a fat envelope of papers into my hand, and then
arresting me as I was stupidly reading them—of course for
spying. What would I do in that case? I think I would pitch
the envelope into the street, shouting, "Don't pull that one
on me, I can't read Russian," and walk away with whatever dignity I had, hoping that would freeze them in their
tracks. A man in danger, if he's walking away from it,
seems indifferent, innocent. At least to himself; then in
my mind I hear the sound of footsteps coming after me,
and since my reveries tend to the rational, two husky
KGB men grab me, shove my arms up my back and
make the arrest. Not for littering the streets, as I hope
might be the case, but for "attempting to dispose of certain
incriminating documents," a fact it's hard to deny.

I see H. Harvitz yelling, squirming, kicking right and
left, till his mouth is shut by somebody's stinking palm and
he is dragged by superior force—not to mention a blackjack
whack on the skull—into the inevitable black Zis I've read
about and see on movie screens.

The cold war is a frightening business, though I suppose for some more than others. I've sometimes wished
spying had reached such a pitch of perfection that both the
U.S.S.R. and the U.S.A. knew everything there is to know
about the other, and having sensibly exchanged this in-
formation by trading computers that keep facts up to date,

let each other alone thereafter. That ruins the spying business; there's that much more sanity in the world, and for a man like me the thought of a trip to the Soviet Union is pure pleasure.

Right away at the Kiev airport I had a sort of fright, after flying in from Paris on a mid-June afternoon. A customs official confiscated from my suitcase five copies of *Visible Secrets*, a poetry anthology for high school students I had edited some years ago, which I had brought along to give away to Russians I met who might be interested in American poetry. I was asked to sign a document the official had carefully written out in Cyrillic, except that *Visible Secrets* was printed in English, "secrets" underlined. The uniformed customs officer, a heavy-set man with a layer of limp hair on a smallish head, red stars on his shoulders, said that the paper I was required to sign stated I understood it was not permitted to bring five copies of a foreign book into the Soviet Union; but I would get my property back anyway at the Moscow airport when I left the country. I worried that I oughtn't to sign but was urged to by my lady Intourist guide, a bleached blonde with wobbly heels whose looks and good humor kept me more or less calm, though my clothes were frankly steaming. She said it was a matter of no great consequence and advised me to write my signature quickly because it was delaying our departure to the Dniepro Hotel.

At that point I asked what would happen if I willingly parted with the books, no longer claimed them as my property. The Intouristka inquired of the customs man, who answered calmly, earnestly, and at great length.

"He says," she said, "that the Soviet Union will not take away from a foreign visitor his legal property."

Since I had only four days in the city and time was going fast, faster than usual, I reluctantly signed the paper plus four carbons—one for each book—or five mysterious government departments?—and was given a copy, which I filed in my billfold.

Despite this incident—it had its comic quality—my stay in Kiev, in spite of the loneliness I usually experience my first few days in a strange city, went quickly and interestingly. In the mornings I was driven around in a private car on guided tours of the hilly, broad-avenued, green-leaved city, whose colors were reminiscent of a subdued Rome. But in the afternoons I wandered around alone. I would start by taking a bus or streetcar, riding a few kilometers, then getting off to walk in this or that neighborhood. Once I strayed into a peasants' market where collective farmers and country folk in beards and boots out of a nineteenth-century Russian novel sold their produce to city people. I thought I must write about this to Rose—I meant of course Lillian. Another time, in a deserted street when I happened to think of the customs receipt in my billfold, I turned in my tracks to see if I were being followed. I wasn't but enjoyed the adventure.

An experience I enjoyed less was getting lost one late afternoon several kilometers above a boathouse on the Dnieper. I was walking along the riverbank liking the boats and island beaches, and before I knew it, had come a good distance from the hotel and was eager to get back because I was hungry. I didn't feel like retracing my route on foot—much too much tourism in three days—so I thought of a cab, and since none was around, maybe an autobus that might be going in the general direction I had come from. I tried approaching a few passers-by whom I addressed in English or pidgin-German, and occasionally trying "Pardonnez-moi"; but the effect was apparently to embarrass them. One young woman ran a few awkward steps from me before she began to walk again. I stepped into an oculist's shop to ask advice of a professional-looking lady in her fifties, wearing pince-nez, a hairnet and white smock. When I addressed her in English, after five seconds of amazement her face froze and she turned her back on me. Hastily thumbing through my guidebook to the phonetic expressions in Russian, I asked, "Gdye hotel?" adding "Dniepro?" To that she gave me an overwrought "Nyet." "Taxi?" I asked. "Nyet," again, this time clapping a hand to her heaving bosom. I figured we'd both had enough and left. Though frustrated, irritated, I spoke to two men passing by, one of whom, the minute he heard my first few words, walked on quickly, his eyes aimed straight ahead, the other indicating by gestures he was deaf and dumb. On impulse I tried him in halting Yiddish that my grandfather had taught me when I was a child, and was then directed, in an undertone in the same language, to a nearby bus stop.

As I was unlocking the door to my room, thinking this was a story I would be telling friends all winter, my phone was ringing. It was a woman's voice. I understood "Go-spodin Garvitz" and one or two other words as she spoke at length in musical Russian. Her voice had the lilt of a singer's. Though I couldn't get the gist of her remarks, I had this sudden vivid reverie, you might call it, of me walking with a pretty Russian girl in a white birchwood near Yasnaya Polyana and coming out of the trees, sincerely talking, into a meadow that sloped to the water; then rowing her around, both of us quiet, in a small lovely lake. It was a peaceful business. I even had thoughts: Wouldn't it be something if I got myself engaged to a Russian girl? That was the general picture, but when the caller was done talking, whatever I had to say I said in English and she slowly hung up.

After breakfast the next morning, she, or somebody who sounded like her—I was aware of a contralto quality —called again.

"If you understood English," I said, "or maybe a little German or French—even Yiddish if you happen to know it —we'd get along fine. But not in Russian, I'm sorry to say. Nyet Russki. I'd be glad to meet you for lunch or whatever you like; so if you get the drift of my remarks why don't you say da? Then dial the English interpreter on extension 37. She could explain to me what's what and we can meet at your convenience."

I had the impression she was listening with both ears, but after a while the phone hung silent in my hand. I wondered where she had got my name, and was someone testing me to find out whether I did or didn't speak Russian. I honestly did not.

Afterward I wrote a short letter to Lillian, telling her I would be leaving for Moscow via Aeroflot, tomorrow at 4 p.m., and I intended to stay there for two weeks, with a break of maybe three or four days in Leningrad, at the Astoria Hotel. I wrote down the exact dates and later air-mailed the letter in a street box some distance from the hotel, whatever good that did. I hoped Lillian would get it in time to reach me by return mail before I left the Soviet Union. To tell the truth I was uneasy all day.

But by the next morning my mood had shifted, and as I was standing at the railing in a park above the Dnieper, looking at the buildings going up across the river in what had once been steppeland, I experienced a curious sense of relief. The vast construction I beheld—it was as though two or three scattered small cities were rising out of the earth —astonished me. This sort of thing was going on all over Russia—halfway around the world—and when I considered what it meant in terms of sheer labor, capital goods, plain morale, I was then and there convinced that the Soviet Union would never willingly provoke a war, nuclear or otherwise, with the United States. Neither would America, in its right mind, with the Soviet Union.

For the first time since I had come to Russia I felt secure and safe, and I enjoyed there, at the breezy railing above the Dnieper, a rare few minutes of euphoria.

Why is it that the most interesting architecture is from Czarist times? I asked myself, and if I'm not mistaken Levitansky quivered, no doubt coincidental. Unless I had spoken aloud to myself, which I sometimes do; I decided I hadn't. We were on our way to the museum, hitting a fast eighty kilometers, which translated to fifty miles an hour was not too bad because traffic was sparse.

"What do you think of my country, the Union of Soviet Socialist Republics?" the driver inquired, turning his head a half circle to see where I was.

"I would appreciate it if you kept your eyes on the road."

"Don't be nervous, I drive now for years."

"I don't like needless risks."

Then I answered I was impressed by much I had seen Obviously it was a great country.

Levitansky's round face appeared in the mirror smiling pleasantly, his teeth eroded. The smile seemed to have appeared from within the mouth. Now that he had revealed his half-Jewish antecedents I had the impression he looked more Jewish than Slavic, and possibly more dissatisfied than I had previously thought. That I got from the eyes.

"Also our system—Communism?"

I answered carefully, not wanting to give offense. "I'll be honest with you. I've seen some unusual things— even inspiring—but my personal taste is for a lot more individual freedom than people seem to have here. America has its serious faults, God knows, but at least we're privileged to criticize, if you know what I mean. My father used to say, 'You can't beat the Bill of Rights.' It's an open society, which means freedom of choice, at least in theory."

"Communism is altogether better political system," Levitansky replied calmly, "although it is not in present stage totally realized. In present stage"—he swallowed, reflected, did not finish the thought. Instead he said, "Our revolution was magnificent and holy event. I love early Soviet history, excitement of Communist idealism, and magnificent victory over bourgeois and imperialist forces. Overnight was lifted up—uplifted—the whole suffering masses. It was born a new life of possibilities for all in society. Pasternak called this 'splendid surgery.' Evgeny Zamyatin—maybe you know his books?—spoke thus: 'The revolution consumes the earth with fire, but then is born a new life.' Many of our poets said similar things."

I didn't argue, each to his revolution.

"You told before," said Levitansky, glancing at me again in the mirror, "that you wish to write articles about your visit. Political or not political?"

"I don't write on politics although interested in it. What I have in mind is something on the literary museums of Moscow for an American travel magazine. That's the sort of thing I do. I'm a free-lance writer." I laughed a little apologetically. It's strange how stresses shift when you're in another country.

Levitansky politely joined in the laugh, stopping in midcourse. "I wish to be certain, what is free-lance writer?"

"Well, an editor might propose an article and I either accept the idea or I don't, or I can write about something that happens to interest me and take my chances I will sell it. Sometimes I don't, and that's so much down the drain financially. What I like about it is I am my own boss. I also edit a bit. I've done anthologies of poetry and essays, both for high school kids."

"We have here free-lance. I am a writer also," Levitansky said solemnly.

"You don't say? You mean as translator?"

"Translation is my profession but I am also original writer."

"Then you do three things to earn a living—write, translate, and drive this cab?"

"The taxi is not my true work."

"Are you translating anything in particular now?"

The driver cleared his throat. "In present time I have no translation project."

"What sort of thing do you write?"

"I write stories."

"Is that so? What kind, if I might ask?"

"I will tell you what kind—little ones—short stories, imagined from life."

"Have you published any?"

He seemed about to turn around to look me in the eye but reached instead into his shirt pocket. I offered my American pack. He shook out a cigarette and lit it, exhaling smoke slowly.

"A few pieces although not recently. To tell the truth" —he sighed—"I write presently for the drawer. You know this expression? Like Isaac Babel, 'I am master of the genre of silence.'"

"I've heard it," I said, not knowing what else to say.

"The mice should read and criticize," Levitansky said

bitterly. "This what they don't eat they make their drops—
droppings—on. It is perfect criticism."

"I'm sorry about that."

"We arrive now to Chekhov Museum."

I leaned forward to pay him and made the impulsive
mistake of adding a one-ruble tip. His face flared. "I am Soviet citizen." He forcibly returned the ruble.

"Call it a thoughtless error," I apologized. "No harm
meant."

"Hiroshima! Nagasaki!" he taunted as the Volga took
off in a burst of smoke. "Aggressor against the suffering
poor people of Vietnam!"

"That's none of my doing," I called after him.

An hour and a half later, after I had signed the guest
book and was leaving the museum, I saw a man standing,
smoking, under a linden tree across the street. Nearby was
a parked taxi. We stared at each other—I wasn't certain at
first who it was, but Levitansky nodded amiably to me,
calling "Welcome! Welcome!" He waved an arm, smiling
open-mouthed. He had combed his thick hair and was
wearing a loose dark suit coat over a tieless white shirt, and
yards of baggy pants. His socks, striped red-white-and-
blue, you could see under his sandals.

I am forgiven, I thought. "Welcome to you," I said,
crossing the street.

"How did you enjoy Chekhov Museum?"

"I did indeed. I've made a lot of notes. You know what

they have there? They have one of his black fedoras, also his pince-nez that you see in pictures of him. Awfully moving."

Levitansky wiped an eye—to my surprise. He seemed not quite the same man, at any rate modified. It's funny, you hear a few personal facts from a stranger and he changes as he speaks. The taxi driver is now a writer, even if part-time. Anyway, that's my dominant impression.

"Excuse me my former anger," Levitansky explained. "Now is not for me the best of times. 'It was the best of times, it was the worst of times,' " he quoted, smiling sadly.

"So long as you pardon my unintentional blunder. Are you perhaps free to drive me to the Metropole or are you here by coincidence?"

I looked around to see if anyone was coming out of the museum.

"If you wish to engage me I will drive you, but at first I wish to show you something—how do you say?—of interest."

He reached through the open front window of the taxi and brought forth a flat package wrapped in brown paper tied with red string.

"Stories which I wrote."

"I don't read Russian," I said.

"My wife has translated of them, four. She is not by her profession a translator, although her English is advanced and sensitive. She had been for two years in England for Soviet Purchasing Commission. We became acquainted in university. I prefer not to translate my own stories because I do not translate so well Russian into English, although I do it beautifully the opposite. Also I will not force myself—it is like self-imitation. Perhaps the stories appear a little awkward in English—also my wife admits this—but you can read and form opinion."

Though he offered the package hesitantly, he offered it as if it were a bouquet of spring flowers. Can it be some sort of trick? I asked myself. Are they testing me because I signed that damned document in the Kiev airport, five copies no less?

Levitansky seemed to know my thought. "It is purely stories."

He bit the string in two, and laying the package on the fender of the Volga, unpeeled the wrapping. There were four stories, clipped separately, typed on long sheets of thin blue paper. I took one Levitansky handed me and scanned the top page—it seemed a story—then I flipped through the other pages and handed the manuscript back. "I'm not much of a critic of stories."

"I don't seek critic. I seek for reader of literary experience and taste. If you have redacted books of poems and also essays, you will be able to judge literary quality of my stories. Please, I request that you will read them."

After a long minute I heard myself say, "Well, I might at that." I didn't recognize the voice and wasn't sure why I had said what I had. You could say I spoke apart from myself, with reluctance that either he wasn't aware of or chose to ignore.

"If you respect—if you approve my stories, perhaps

you will be able to arrange for publication in Paris or either London?" His larynx wobbled.

I stared at the man. "I don't happen to be going to Paris, and I'll be in London only between planes to the U.S.A."

"In this event, perhaps you will show to your publisher, and he will publish my work in America?" Levitansky was now visibly uneasy.

"In America?" I said, raising my voice in disbelief.

For the first time he gazed around cautiously before replying.

"If you will be so kind to show them to publisher of your books—he is reliable publisher?—perhaps he will wish to put out volume of my stories? I will make contract whatever he will like. Money, if I could get, is not an ideal."

"Whatever volume are you talking about?"

He said that from thirty stories he had written he had chosen eighteen, of which these four were a sample. "Unfortunately more are not now translated. My wife is biochemist assistant and works long hours in laboratory. I am sure your publisher will enjoy to read these. It will depend on your opinion."

Either this man has a fantastic imagination or he's out of his right mind. "I wouldn't want to get myself involved in smuggling a Russian manuscript out of Russia."

"I have informed you that my manuscript is of made-up stories."

"That may be but it's still a chancy enterprise. I'd be taking chances I have no desire to take, to be frank."

"At least if you will read," he sighed.

I took the stories again and thumbed slowly through each. What I was looking for I couldn't say: maybe a booby trap? Should I or shouldn't I? I thought. Why should I?

He handed me the wrapping paper and I rolled up the stories in it. The quicker I read them, the quicker I've read them. I got into the cab.

"As I said, I'm at the Metropole. Come by tonight about nine o'clock and I'll give you my opinion for what it's worth. But I'm afraid I'll have to limit it to that, Mr. Levitansky, without further obligation or expectations, or it's no deal. My room number is 538."

"Tonight?—so soon?" he said, scratching both palms. "You must read with care so you will realize the art."

"Tomorrow night, then, same time. I'd rather not have them in my room longer than that."

Levitansky agreed. Whistling softly through his eroded teeth, he drove me carefully to the Metropole.

That night, sipping vodka from a drinking glass, I read Levitansky's stories. They were simply and strongly written—I had almost expected it—and not badly translated; in fact the translation read much better than I had been led to think although there were of course some gaffes—odd constructions, ill-fitting stiff words, some indicated by question marks, and taken, I suppose, from a thesaurus. And the stories, short tales dealing—somewhat to my surprise—mostly with Moscow Jews, were good, artistically done, really moving. The situations they revealed weren't exactly news to me: I'm a careful reader of

The Times. But the stories weren't written to complain.
What they had to say was achieved as form, no telling the
dancer from the dance. I poured myself another glass of
the potato potion—I was beginning to feel high, occasionally wondering why I was putting so much away—
relaxing, I guess. I then reread the stories with admiration
for Levitansky. I had the feeling he was no ordinary man.
I felt excited, then depressed, as if I had been let in on a
secret I didn't want to know.

It's a hard life here for a fiction writer, I thought.

Afterward, having the stories around made me uneasy.
In one of them a Russian writer burns his stories in the
kitchen sink. Obviously nobody had burned these. I
thought to myself, If I'm caught with them in my posses-
sion, considering what they indicate about conditions here,
there's no question I'll be up to my hips in trouble. I wish I
had insisted that Levitansky come back for them tonight.

There was a solid rap on the door. I felt I had risen a
good few inches out of my chair. It was, after a while,
Levitansky.

"Out of the question," I said, thrusting the stories at
him. "Absolutely out of the question!"

The next night we sat facing each other over glasses of
cognac in the writer's small, book-crowded study. He was
dignified, at first haughty, wounded, hardly masking his
impatience. I wasn't myself exactly comfortable.

I had come out of courtesy and other considerations, I

guess; principally a dissatisfaction I couldn't exactly define, except it tied up with the kind of man I am or want to be, the self that sometimes gets me involved in matters I don't like to get involved in—always a dangerous business.

Levitansky, the taxi driver rattling around in his Volga–Pegasus, amateur trying to palm off a half-ass ms., had faded in my mind, and I saw him now as a serious Soviet writer with publishing problems. There are others. What can I do for him? I thought. Why should I?

"I didn't express what I really felt last night," I apologized. "You caught me by surprise, I'm sorry to say."

Levitansky was scratching each hand with the blunt fingers of the other. "How did you acquire my address?"

I reached into my pocket for a wad of folded brown wrapping paper. "It's on this—Novo Ostapovskaya Street, 488, Flat 59. I took a cab."

"I had forgotten this."

Maybe, I thought.

Still, I had practically had to put my foot in the door to get in. Levitansky's wife had answered my uncertain knock, her eyes worried, an expression I took to be the one she lived with. The eyes, astonished to behold a stranger, became outright hostile once I had inquired in English for her husband. I felt, as in Kiev, that my native tongue had become my enemy.

"Have you not the wrong apartment?"

"I hope not. Not if Gospodin Levitansky lives here. I came to see him about his—ah—manuscript."

Her startled eyes darkened as her face paled. Ten

seconds later I was in the flat, the door locked behind me.

"Levitansky!" she summoned him. It had a reluctant quality: Come but don't come.

He appeared in apparently the same shirt, pants, tricolor socks. There was at first pretend-boredom in a tense, tired face. He could not, however, conceal excitement, his lit eyes roving, returning, roving.

"Oh ho," Levitansky said, whatever it meant.

My God, I thought, has he been expecting me?

"I came to talk to you for a few minutes, if you don't mind," I said. "I want to say what I really think of the stories you kindly let me read."

He curtly spoke in Russian to his wife and she snapped an answer back. "I wish to introduce my wife, Irina Filipovna Levitansky, biochemist. She is patient although not a saint."

She smiled tentatively, an attractive woman about twenty-eight, a little on the hefty side, in house slippers and plain dress. The edge of her slip hung below her skirt.

There was a touch of British in her accent. "I am pleased to be acquainted." If so one hardly noticed. She stepped into black pumps and slipped a bracelet on her wrist, a lit cigarette dangling from the corner of her mouth. Her legs and arms were shapely, her brown hair cut short. I had the impression of tight thin lips in a pale face.

"I will go to Kovalevsky, next door," she said.

"Not on my account, I hope? All I have to say—"

"Our neighbors in the next flat," Levitansky grimaced. "Also thin walls." He knocked a knuckle on a hollow wall.

I indicated my dismay.

"Please, not long," Irina said, "because I am afraid."

Surely not of me? Agent Howard Harvitz, C.I.A.—a comical thought.

Their small square living room wasn't unattractive but Levitansky signaled the study inside. He offered sweet cognac in whiskey tumblers, then sat facing me at the edge of his chair, repressed energy all but visible. I had the momentary sense his chair was about to move, fly off.

If it does he goes alone.

"What I came to say," I told him, "is that I like your stories and am sorry I didn't say so last night. I like the primary, close-to-the-bone quality of the writing. The stories impress me as strong if simply wrought; I appreciate your feeling for people and at the same time the objectivity with which you render them. It's sort of Chekhovian in quality, but more compressed, sinewy, direct, if you know what I mean. For instance, that story about the old father coming to see his son who ducks out on him. I can't comment on your style, having only read the stories in translation."

"Chekhovian," Levitansky admitted, smiling through his worn teeth, "is fine compliment. Mayakovsky, our early Soviet poet, described him 'the strong and gay artist of the word.' I wish it was possible for Levitansky to be so gay in life and art." He seemed to be staring at the drawn shade in the room, though maybe no place in particular, then said, perhaps heartening himself, "In Russian is magnificent my style—precise, economy, including wit. The style is difficult to translate in English because is less rich language."

"I've heard that said. In fairness I should add I have some reservations about the stories, yet who hasn't on any given piece of creative work?"

"I have myself reservations."

The admission made, I skipped the criticism. I had been wondering about a picture on his bookcase and then asked who it was. "It's a face I've seen before. The eyes are poetic, you might say."

"So is the voice. This is picture of Boris Pasternak as young man. On the wall yonder is Mayakovsky. He was also remarkable poet, wild, joyful, neurasthenic, a lover of the Revolution. He spoke: 'This is *my* Revolution.' To him was it 'a holy washerwoman who cleaned off all the filth from the earth.' Unfortunately he was later disillusioned and shot himself."

"I read that."

"He wrote: 'I wish to be understood by my country—but if no, I will fly through Russia like a slanting rainstorm.'"

"Have you by chance read *Dr. Zhivago?*"

"I have read," the writer sighed, and then began to declaim in Russian—I guessed some lines from a poem.

"It is to Marina Tsvetayeva, Soviet poetess, good friend of Pasternak." Levitansky fiddled with the pack of cigarettes on the table. "The end of her life was unfortunate."

"Is there no picture of Osip Mandelstam?" I hesitated as I spoke the name.

He reacted as though he had just met me. "You know Mandelstam?"

"Just a few poems in an anthology."

"Our best poet—he is holy—gone with so many others. My wife does not let me hang his photograph."

"I guess why I really came," I said after a minute, "is I wanted to express my sympathy and respect."

Levitansky popped a match with his thumbnail. His hand trembled, so he shook the flame out without lighting the cigarette.

Embarrassed for him, I pretended to be looking elsewhere. "It's a small room. Does your son sleep here?"

"Don't confuse my story of writer, which you have read, with life of author. My wife and I are married eight years though without children."

"Might I ask whether the experience you describe in that same story—the interview with the editor—was true?"

"Not true although truth," the writer said impatiently. "I write from imagination. I am not interested to repeat contents of diaries or total memory."

"On that I go along."

"Also, which is not in story, I have submitted to Soviet journals sketches and tales many many times but only few have been published, although not my best. Some people, but also few, know my work through samizdat, which is passing from one to another the manuscript."

"Did you submit any of the Jewish stories?"

"Please, stories are stories, they have not nationality."

"I mean by that those about Jews."

"Some I have submitted but they were not accepted."

Brave man, I thought. "After reading the four you gave me, I wondered how it is you write so well about Jews? You call yourself a marginal one—I believe that was your word—yet you write with authority about them. Not that one can't, I suppose, but it's surprising when one does."

"Imagination makes authority. When I write about Jews comes out stories, so I write about Jews. I write on subjects that make for me stories. Is not important that I am half-Jew. What is important is observation, feeling, also the art. In the past I have observed my Jewish father. Also I study sometimes Jews in the synagogue. I sit there on the bench for strangers. The gabbai watches me with dark eyes and I watch him. But whatever I write, whether is about Jews, Galicians, or Georgians, must be work of invention or for me it does not live."

"I'm not much of a synagogue-goer myself," I told him, "but I like to drop in once in a while to be refreshed by the language and images of a time and place where God was. That's funny because I have no religious education to speak of."

"I am atheist."

"I understand what you mean by imagination—that praying-shawl story. But am I right"—I lowered my voice—"that you are saying also something about the condition of Jews in this country?"

"I do not make propaganda," Levitansky said sternly. "I am not Israeli spokesman. I am Soviet artist."

"I didn't mean you weren't but there's a strong sympathy for Jews, and, after all, ideas are born in life."

"My purpose belongs to me."

"One senses an awareness of injustice."

"Whatever is the injustice, the product must be art."

"Well, I respect your philosophy."

"Please do not respect so much," the writer said irritably. "We have in my country a quotation: 'It is impossible to make out of apology a fur coat.' The idea is similar. I appreciate your respect but need now practical assistance."

Expecting words of the sort I started to say something noncommittal.

"Listen at first to me," Levitansky said, slapping the table with his palm. "I am in desperate condition—situation. I have written for years but little is published. In the past, one—two editors who were friendly told me, private, that my stories are excellent but I violate social realism. This what you call objectivity they called it excessive naturalism and sentiment. It is hard to listen to such nonsense. They advise me swim but not to use my legs. They have warned me; also they have made excuses for me which I do not like them. Even they said I am crazy although I explained them I submit my stories *because* Soviet Union is great country. A great country does not fear what artist writes. A great country breathes into its lungs work of writers, painters, musicians, and becomes more great, more healthy. That I told to them but they replied I am not sufficient realist. This is the reason I am not invited to be member of Writers Union. Without this is impossible to be published." He smiled sourly. "They have warned me to stop submitting to journals my work, so I have stopped."

"I'm sorry about that," I said. "I don't myself believe any good comes from exiling the poets."

"I cannot continue longer any more in this fashion," Levitansky said, laying his hand on his heart. "I feel I am locked in drawer with my poor stories. Now I must get out or I suffocate. It becomes for me each day more difficult to write. I need help. It is not easy to request a stranger for such important personal favor. My wife advised me not. She is angry, also frightened, but it is impossible to go on in this way. I am convinced I am important Soviet writer. I must have audience. I wish to see my books to be read by Soviet people. I wish to have in minds different than my own and my wife acknowledgment of my art. I wish them to know my work is related to Russian writers of the past as well as modern. I am in tradition of Chekhov, Gorky, Isaac Babel. I know if book of my stories will be published, it will make for me fine reputation. This is reason why you must help me—it is necessary for my interior liberty."

His confession came in an agitated burst. I use the word advisedly because that's partly what upset me. I have never cared for confessions such as are meant to involve unwilling people in others' personal problems. Russians are past masters of the art—you can see it in their novels.

"I appreciate the honor of your request," I said, "but all I am is a passing tourist. That's a pretty tenuous relationship between us."

"I do not ask tourist—I ask human being—man," Levitansky said passionately. "Also you are free-lance writer. You know now what I am and what is on my heart. You sit in my house. Who else can I ask? I would prefer to publish in Europe my stories, maybe with Mondadori or Einaudi in Italy, but if this is impossible to you I will publish in America. Someday will my work be read in my own country, maybe after I am dead. This is terrible irony but my generation lives on such ironies. Since I am not now ambitious to die it will be great relief to me to know that at least in one language is alive my art. Mandelstam wrote: 'I will be enclosed in some alien speech.' Better so than nothing."

"You say I know who you are but do you know who *I* am?" I asked him. "I'm a plain person, not very imaginative though I don't write a bad article. My whole life, for some reason, has been without much real adventure, except I was divorced once and remarried happily to a woman whose death I am still mourning. Now I'm here more or less on a vacation, not to jeopardize myself by taking serious chances of an unknown sort. What's more—and this is the main thing I came to tell you—I wouldn't at all be surprised if I am already under suspicion and would do you more harm than good."

I told Levitansky about the airport incident in Kiev. "I signed a document I couldn't even read, which was a foolish thing to do."

"In Kiev this happened?"

"That's right."

He laughed dismally. "It would not happen to you if

you entered through Moscow. In the Ukraine—what is your word?—they are rubes, country people."

"That might be—nevertheless I signed the paper."

"Do you have copy?"

"Not with me. In my desk drawer in the hotel."

"I am certain this is receipt for your books which officials will return to you when you depart from Soviet Union."

"That's what I'd be afraid of."

"Why afraid?" he asked. "Are you afraid to receive back umbrella which you have lost?"

"I'd be afraid one thing might lead to another—more questions, other searches. It would be stupid to have your manuscript in my suitcase, in Russian, no less, that I can't even read. Suppose they accuse me of being some kind of courier transferring stolen documents?"

The thought raised me to my feet. I then realized the tension in the room was thick as steam, mostly mine.

Levitansky rose, embittered. "There is no question of spying. I do not think I have presented myself as traitor to my country."

"I didn't say anything of the sort. All I'm saying is I don't want to get into trouble with the Soviet authorities. Nobody can blame me for that. In other words the enterprise isn't for me."

"I have made inquirings," Levitansky insisted. "You will have nothing to fear for tourist who has been a few weeks in U.S.S.R. under guidance of Intourist and does not speak Russian. My wife said to me your baggage will not be further inspected. They sometimes do so to political people, also to bourgeois journalists who have made bad impression. I would deliver to you the manuscript in the last instance. It is typed on less than one hundred fifty sheets thin paper and will make small package, weightless. If it should look to you like trouble you can leave it in dustbin. My name will not be anywhere and if they find it and track—trace to me the stories, I will answer I have thrown them out myself. They won't believe this but what other can I say? It will make no difference anyway. If I stop my writing I may as well be dead. No harm will come to you."

"I'd rather not if you don't mind."

With what I guess was a curse of despair, Levitansky reached for the portrait on his bookcase and flung it against the wall. Pasternak struck Mayakovsky, splattering him with glass, shattering himself, and both pictures crashed to the floor.

"Free-lance writer," he shouted, "go to hell to America! Tell to Negroes about Bill of Rights! Tell them they are free although you keep them slaves! Talk to sacrificed Vietnamese people that you respect them!"

Irina Filipovna entered the room on the run. "Feliks," she entreated, "Kovalevsky hears every word!"

"Please," she begged me, "please go away. Leave poor Levitansky alone. I beg you from my miserable heart."

I left in a hurry. The next day I left for Leningrad.

Three days later, not exactly at my best after a tense visit to Leningrad, I was sitting loosely in a beat-up taxi with a cheerful Intouristka, a half hour after my arrival at the Moscow airport. We were driving to the Ukraine Hotel, where I was assigned for my remaining days in the Soviet Union. I would have preferred the Metropole again because it is so conveniently located and I was used to it, but on second thought, better some place where a certain party wouldn't know I lived. The Volga we were riding in seemed somehow familiar, but if so it was safely in the hands of a small stranger with a large wool cap, a man wearing sunglasses who paid me no particular attention.

I had had a rather special several minutes in Leningrad on my first day. On a white summer's evening, shortly after I had unpacked in my room at the Astoria, I discovered the Winter Palace and Hermitage after a walk along Nevsky Prospekt. Chancing on Palace Square, vast, deserted at the moment, I felt an unexpected intense emotion in thinking of the revolutionary events that had occurred on this spot. My God, I thought, why should I feel myself part of Russian history? It's a contagious business, what happens to men. On the Palace Bridge I gazed at the ice-blue Neva, in the distance the golden steeple of the cathedral built by Peter the Great, gleaming under masses of wind-driven clouds in patches of green sky. It's the Soviet Union but it's still Russia.

The next day I woke up anxious. In the street I was approached twice by strangers speaking English; I think my suede shoes attracted them. The first, tight-eyed and badly dressed, wanted to sell me black-market rubles. "Nyet," I said, tipping my straw hat and hurrying on. The second, a tall, bearded boy of about nineteen, with a left-sided tuft longer than right, wearing a home-knitted green pullover, offered to buy jazz records, "youth clothes," and American cigarettes. "Sorry, nothing for sale." I escaped him too, except that green sweater followed me for a kilometer along one of the canals. I broke into a run. When I looked back he had disappeared. I slept badly—it stayed light too long past midnight; and in the morning inquired about the possibility of an immediate flight to Helsinki. I was informed I couldn't book one for a week. Calming myself, I decided to return to Moscow a day before I had planned to, mostly to see what they had in the Dostoevsky Museum.

I had been thinking a good deal about Levitansky. How much of a writer was he really? I had read four of eighteen stories he wanted to publish. Suppose he had showed me the best and the others were mediocre or thereabouts? Was it worth taking a chance for that kind of book? I thought, the best thing for my peace of mind is to forget the guy. Before checking out of the Astoria I received a chatty letter from Lillian, forwarded from Moscow, apparently not in response to my recent one to her but written earlier. Should I marry her? Did I dare? The phone rang piercingly, but when I picked up the receiver no one answered. On the plane to Moscow I had visions of a crash; there must be many in the Soviet Union nobody ever reads of.

In my room on the twelfth floor of the Ukraine I relaxed in a green plastic-covered armchair. There was also a single low bed and a utilitarian pinewood desk, an apple-green telephone plunked on it for instant use. I'll be home in a week, I thought. Now I'd better shave and see if anything is left in the way of a concert or opera ticket for tonight. I'm in a mood for music.

The electric plug in the bathroom didn't work, so I put away my shaver and was lathering up when I jumped to a single explosive knock on the door. I opened it cautiously and there stood Levitansky with a brown paper packet in his hand.

Is this son-of-a-bitch out to compromise me?

"How did you happen to find out where I was only twenty minutes after I got here, Mr. Levitansky?"

"How I found you?" the writer shrugged. He seemed deathly tired, the face longer, leaner, resembling a hungry fox on his last unsteady legs but still in business.

"My brother-in-law was chauffeur for you from the airport. He heard the girl inquire your name. We have spoke of you. Dmitri—this is my wife's brother—informed me you have registered at the Ukraine. I inquired downstairs your room number and it was granted to me."

"However it happened," I said firmly, "I want you to know I haven't changed my mind. I don't want to get more involved. I thought it all through while I was in Leningrad and that's my final decision."

"I may come in?"

"Please, but for obvious reasons I'd appreciate a short visit."

Levitansky sat, somewhat shriveled, thin knees

pressed together, in the armchair, his parcel awkwardly on his lap. If he was happy he had found me it did nothing for his expression.

I finished shaving, put on a fresh white shirt, and sat down on the bed. "Sorry I have nothing to offer in the way of an aperitif but I could call downstairs?"

Levitansky twiddled his fingers no. He was dressed without change down to his socks. Did his wife wash out the same pair every night or were all his socks red-white-and-blue?

"To speak frankly," I said, "I have to protest this constant tension you've whipped up in and around me. Nobody in his right mind can expect a complete stranger visiting the Soviet Union to pull his chestnuts out of the fire. It's your country that's hindering you as a writer, not me or the United States of America, and since you live here what can you do but live with it?"

"I love my country," Levitansky said.

"Nobody denies that. So do I love mine, though love for country—let's face it—is a mixed bag of marbles. Nationality isn't soul, as I'm sure you agree. But what I'm also saying is there are things about his country one might not like that he has to make his peace with. I'm assuming you're not thinking of counter-revolution. So if you're up against a wall you can't climb or dig under or outflank, at least stop banging your head against it, not to mention mine. Do what you can. It's amazing, for instance, what can be said in a fairy tale."

"I have written already my fairy tales," Levitansky

said moodily. "Now is the time for truth without disguises. I will make my peace to this point where it interferes with work of my imagination—my interior liberty; and then I must stop to make my peace. My brother-in-law has also told to me, 'You must write acceptable stories, others can do it, so why cannot you?' And I have answered to him, 'They must be acceptable to *me!*' "

"In that case, aren't you up against the impossible? If you permit me to say it, are those Jews in your stories, if they can't have their matzos and prayer books, any freer in their religious lives than you are as a writer? That's what you're really saying when you write about them. What I mean is, one has to face up to the nature of his society."

"I have faced up. Do you face up to yours?" he asked with a flash of scorn.

"Not as well as I might. My own problem is not that I can't express myself but that I don't. In my own mind Vietnam is a horrifying and demoralizing mistake, yet I've never really opposed it except to sign a couple of petitions and vote for congressmen who say they're against the war. My first wife used to criticize me. She said I wrote the wrong things and was involved in everything but useful action. My second wife knew this but made me think she didn't. In a curious way I'm just waking up to the fact that the United States Government has for years been mucking up my soul."

From the heat of my body I could tell I was blushing.

Levitansky's large larynx moved up like a flag on a pole, then sank wordlessly.

He tried again, saying, "The Soviet Union preservates for us the great victories of our revolution. Because of this I have remained for years at peace with the State. Communism is still to me inspirational ideal although this historical period is spoiled by leaders with impoverished view of humanity. They have pissed on revolution."

"Stalin?"

"Him especially but also others. Even so I have obeyed Party directives, and when I could not longer obey I wrote for drawer. I said to myself, 'Levitansky, history changes every minute and also Communism will change.' I believed if the State restricts two, three generations of artists, what is this against development of true socialist society—maybe best society of world history? So what does it mean if some of us are sacrificed to Party purpose? The aesthetic mode is not in necessity greater than politics —than needs of revolution. And what if are suppressed two generations of artists? Therefore will be so much less bad books, poor painting, bad music. Then in fifty years more will be secure the State and all Soviet artists will say whatever they wish. This is what I thought, or tried to think, but do not longer think so. I do not believe more in partiinost, which is guided thought, an expression which is to me ridiculous. I do not believe in bolshevization of literature. I do not think revolution is fulfilled in country of unpublished novelists, poets, playwriters, who hide in drawers whole libraries of literature that will never be printed, or if so, it will be printed after they stink in their graves. I think now the State will never be secure—

never! It is not in the nature of politics, or human condition, to be finished with revolution. Evgeny Zamyatin told: 'There is no final revolution. Revolutions are infinite!' "

"I guess that's along my own line of thinking," I said, hoping for reasons of personal safety to forestall Levitansky's ultimate confession—one he, with brooding eyes, was already relentlessly making—lest in the end it imprison me in his will and history.

"I have learned from writing my stories," the writer was saying, "that imagination is enemy of the State. I have learned from my writing that I am not free man. This is my conclusion. I ask for your help, not to harm my country, which still has magnificent socialistic possibilities, but to help me escape its worst errors. I do not wish to defame Russia. My purpose in my work is to show its true heart. So have done our writers from Pushkin to Pasternak and also, in his way, Solzhenitsyn. If you believe in democratic humanism you must help artist to be free. Is not true?"

I got up, I think to shake myself free of that question. "What exactly is my responsibility to you, Levitansky?" I tried to contain the exasperation I felt.

"We are members of mankind. If I am drowning you must assist to save me."

"In unknown waters if I can't swim?"

"If not, throw to me rope."

"I'm a visitor here. I've told you I may be suspect. For all I know you yourself might be a Soviet agent out to get me, or the room may be bugged and then where are we? Mr. Levitansky, please, I don't want to hear or argue any more. I'll just plead personal inability and ask you to leave."

"Bugged?"

"Some sort of listening device planted in this room."

Levitansky slowly turned gray. He sat a moment in motionless meditation, then rose wearily from the chair.

"I withdraw now request for your assistance. I accept your word that you are not capable. I do not wish to make criticism of you. All I wish to say, Gospodin Garvitz, is it requires more to change a man's character than to change his name."

Levitansky left the room, leaving in his wake faint fumes of cognac. He had also passed gas.

"Come back!" I called, not too loudly, but if he heard through the door he didn't answer. Good riddance, I thought. Not that I don't sympathize with him but look what he's done to *my* interior liberty. Who has to come thousands of miles to Russia to get caught up in this kind of mess? It's a helluva way to spend a vacation.

The writer had gone but not his sneaky manuscript. It was lying on my bed.

"It's his baby, not mine." Angered, I knotted my tie and slipped on my coat, then via the English-language number, called a cab. But I had forgotten his address. A half hour later I was still in the taxi, riding anxiously back and forth along Novo Ostapovskaya Street until I spotted the apartment house I thought it might be. It wasn't, it was another like it. I paid the driver and walked on till once again I thought I had the house. After going up the stairs I was sure it was. When I knocked on Levitansky's door, the writer, looking older, more distant—as if he'd been away on a trip and had just returned; or maybe simply interrupted at his work, his thoughts still in his words on the page on the table, his pen in hand—stared blankly at me. Very blankly.

"Levitansky, my heart breaks for you, I swear, but I can't take the chance. I believe in you but am not, at this time of my life, considering my condition and recent experiences, in much of a mood to embark on a dangerous adventure. Please accept deepest regrets."

I thrust the manuscript into his hand and rushed down the stairs. Hurrying out of the building, I was, to my horror, unable to avoid Irina Levitansky coming in. Her eyes lit in fright as she recognized me an instant before I hit her full force and sent her sprawling along the walk.

"Oh, my God, what have I done? I beg your pardon!" I helped the dazed, hurt woman to her feet, brushing off her soiled skirt, and futilely, her pink blouse, split and torn on her lacerated arm and shoulder. I stopped dead when I felt myself experiencing erotic sensations.

Irina Filipovna held a handkerchief to her bloody nostril and wept a little. We sat on a stone bench, a girl of ten and her little brother watching us. Irina said something to them in Russian and they moved off.

"I was frightened of you also as you are of us," she said. "I trust you now because Levitansky does. But I will not urge you to take the manuscript. The responsibility is for you to decide."

"It's not a responsibility I want," I said unhappily.

She said as though to herself, "Maybe I will leave Levitansky. He is wretched so much it is no longer a marriage. He drinks. Also he does not earn a living. My brother Dmitri allows him to drive the taxi two, three hours of the day, to my brother's disadvantage. Except for a ruble or two from this, I support him. Levitansky does not longer receive translation commissions. Also a neighbor in the house—I am sure Kovalevsky—has denounced him to the police for delinquency and parasitism. There will be a hearing. Levitansky says he will burn his manuscripts."

"Good God, I've just returned the package of stories!"

"He will not," she said. "But even if he burns he will write more. If they take him away in prison he will write on toilet paper. When he comes out, he will write on newspaper margins. He sits this minute at his table. He is a magnificent writer. I cannot ask him not to write, but now I must decide if this is the condition I wish for myself for the rest of my life."

Irina sat in silence, an attractive woman with shapely legs and feet, in a soiled skirt and torn blouse. I left her on the stone bench, her handkerchief squeezed in her fist.

That night—July 2, I was leaving the Soviet Union on the fifth—I experienced massive self-doubt. If I'm a coward why has it taken so long to find out? Where does anxiety end and cowardice begin? Feelings get mixed, sure enough, but not all cowards are anxious men, and not all anxious men are cowards. Many "sensitive" (Rose's word), tense, even frightened human beings did in fear what had to be done, the fear calling up energy when it's time to fight or jump off a rooftop into a river. There comes a time in a man's life when to get where he has to go—if there are no doors or windows—he walks through a wall.

On the other hand, suppose one is courageous in a foolish cause—you concentrate on courage and not enough on horse sense? To get to the point of the problem endlessly on my mind, how do I finally decide it's a sensible and worthwhile thing to smuggle out Levitansky's manuscript, given my reasonable doubts of the ultimate worth of the operation? Granted, as I now grant, he's a trustworthy guy and his wife is that and more; still, does it pay a man like me to run the risk?

If six thousand Soviet writers can't do very much to squeeze out another inch of freedom as artists, who am I to fight their battle—H. Harvitz, knight-of-the-free-lance from Manhattan? How far do you go, granted all men, including Communists, are created free and equal and justice is for all? How far do you go for art, if you're for Yeats, Matisse, and Ludwig van Beethoven? Not to mention Gogol, Tolstoy, and Dostoevsky. So far as to get yourself intentionally involved: the HH Ms. Smuggling Service? Will the President and State Department send up three loud cheers for my contribution to the cause of artistic social justice? And suppose it amounts to no more than a gaffe in the end?—What will I prove if I sneak out Levitansky's manuscript and all it turns out to be is just another passable book of stories?

That's how I argued with myself on more than one occasion, but in the end I argued myself into solid indecision.

What it boils down to, I'd say, is he expects me to help him because I'm an American. That's quite a nerve.

Two nights later—odd not to have the Fourth of July on July 4 (I was listening for firecrackers)—a quiet light-lemon summer's evening in Moscow, after two monotonously uneasy days, though I was still writing museum notes, for relief I took myself off to the Bolshoi to hear *Tosca*. It was sung in Russian by a busty lady and handsome tenor, but the Italian plot was unchanged, and in the end, Scarpia, who had promised "death" by fake bullets, gave in sneaky exchange a fusillade of hot lead; another artist bit the dust and Floria Tosca learned the hard way that love wasn't what she had thought.

Next to me sat another full-breasted woman, this one a lovely Russian of maybe thirty in a white dress that fitted a well-formed mature figure, her blond hair piled in a birdlike mass on her splendid head. Lillian could look like that, though not Rose. This woman—alone, it turned out—spoke flawless English in a mezzo-soprano with a slight accent.

During the first intermission she asked in friendly fashion, managing to seem detached but interested: "Are you American? Or perhaps Swedish?"

"Not Swedish. American is correct. How did you happen to guess?"

"I noticed, if it does not bother you that I say it," she remarked with a charming laugh, "a certain self-satisfaction."

"You got the wrong party," I said.

When she opened her purse a fragrance of springtime

burst forth—fresh flowers; the warmth of her body rose to my nostrils. I was moved by memories of the hungers of youth—dreams, longing.

During intermission she touched my arm and said in a low voice, "May I ask a favor? Do you depart from the Soviet Union?"

"In fact tomorrow."

"How fortunate for me. Would it offer too much difficulty to mail wherever you are going an airmail letter addressed to my husband, who is presently in Paris? Our airmail service takes two weeks to arrive in the West. I shall be grateful."

I glanced at the envelope addressed half in French, half in Cyrillic, and said I wouldn't mind. But during the next act sweat grew active on my flesh and at the end of the opera, after Tosca's shriek of suicide, I handed the letter back to the not wholly surprised lady, saying I was sorry. Nodding to her, I left the theater. I had the feeling I had heard her voice before. I hurried back to the hotel, determined not to leave my room for any reason other than breakfast, then out and into the wide blue sky.

I later fell asleep over a book and a bottle of sweetish warm beer a waiter had brought up, pretending to myself I was relaxed though I was as usual concerned beforehand with worried thoughts of the departure and flight home; and when I awoke, three minutes on my wristwatch later, it seemed to me I had made the acquaintance of a spate of new nightmares. I was momentarily panicked by the idea that someone had planted a letter on me, and I searched through the pockets of my two suits. Nyet. Then

I recalled that in one of my dreams a drawer in a table I was sitting at had slowly come open and Feliks Levitansky, a dwarf who lived in it along with a few friendly mice, managed to scale the wooden wall on the comb he used as a ladder, and to hop from the drawer ledge to the top of the table. He leered into my face, shook his Lilliputian fist, and shouted in high-pitched but (to me) understandable Russian, "Atombombnik! You massacred innocent Japanese people! Amerikansky bastards!"

"That's unfair," I cried out. "I was no more than a kid in college."

That's a sad dream, I thought.

Afterwards this occurred to me: Suppose what happened to Levitansky happens to me. Suppose America gets caught up in a war with China in some semi-reluctant stupid way, and to make fast hash of it—despite my frantic loud protestations: mostly I wave my arms and shout obscenities till my face turns green—we spatter them, before they can get going, with a few dozen H-bombs, boiling up a thick atomic soup of about two hundred million Orientals —blood, gristle, marrow, and lots of floating Chinese eyeballs. We win the war because the Soviets hadn't been able to make up their minds who to shoot their missiles at first. And suppose after this unheard-of slaughter, about ten million Americans, in self-revulsion, head for the borders to flee the country. To stop the loss of wealth, the refugees are intercepted by the army in tanks and turned back. Harvitz hides in his room with shades drawn, writing in a fury of protest a long epic poem condemning the mass butchery by America. What nation, Asiatic or other, is next? Nobody in the States wants to publish the poem because it might start riots and another flight of refugees to Canada and Mexico; then one day there's a knock on the door, and it isn't the F.B.I. but a bearded Levitansky, in better times a Soviet tourist, a modern, not medieval Communist. He kindly offers to sneak the manuscript of the poem out for publication in the Soviet Union.

Why? Harvitz suspiciously asks.

Why not? To give the book its liberty.

I awoke after a restless night. I had been instructed by Intourist to be in the lobby with my baggage two hours before flight time at 11 a.m. I was shaved and dressed by six, and at seven had breakfast—I was very hungry—of yogurt, sausage, and scrambled eggs in the twelfth-floor buffet. I then went out to hunt for a taxi. They were hard to come by at this hour but I finally located one near the American Embassy, not far from the hotel. Speaking my usual mixture of primitive German and French, I persuaded the driver by first suggesting, then slipping him an acceptable two rubles, to take me to Levitansky's house and wait a few minutes till I came out. Going hastily up the stairs, I knocked on his door, apologizing when he opened it, to the half-pajamaed, iron-faced writer, for awaking him this early in the day. Without peace of mind or certainty of purpose I asked him whether he still wanted me to smuggle out his manuscript of stories. I got for my trouble the door slammed in my face.

A half hour later I had everything packed and was locking the suitcase. A knock on the door—half a rap, you might call it. For the suitcase, I thought. I was momen-

tarily frightened by the sight of a small man in a thick cap
wearing a long trench coat. He winked, and against the
will I winked back. I had recognized Levitansky's brother-
in-law Dmitri, the taxi driver. He slid in, unbuttoned his
coat, and brought forth the wrapped manuscript. Holding
a finger to his lips, he handed it to me before I could say
I was no longer interested.

"Levitansky changed his mind?"

"Not changed mind. Was afraid your voice to be heard
by Kovalevsky."

"I'm sorry, I should have thought of that."

"Levitansky say not write to him," the brother-in-law
whispered. "When is published book please send to him
copy of *Das Kapital*. He will understand message."

I reluctantly agreed.

The brother-in-law, a short shapeless figure with sad
Jewish eyes, winked again, shook hands with a steamy
palm, and slipped out of my room.

I unlocked my suitcase and laid the manuscript on top
of my shirts. Then I unpacked half the contents and slipped
the manuscript into a folder containing my notes on literary
museums and a few letters from Lillian. I then and there
decided that if I got back to the States, the next time I
saw her I would ask her to marry me. The phone was
ringing as I left the room.

On my way to the airport, alone in a taxi—no Intourist
girl accompanied me—I felt, on and off, nauseated. If it's
not the sausage and yogurt it must just be ordinary fear.
Still, if Levitansky has the courage to send these stories out
the least I can do is give him a hand. When one thinks of

it it's little enough he does for human freedom in the course of his life. At the airport if I can dig up a bromo or its Russian equivalent I know I'll feel better.

The driver was observing me in the mirror, a stern man with the head of a scholar, impassively smoking.

"Le jour fait beau," I said.

He pointed with an upraised finger to a sign in English at one side of the road to the airport:

"Long live peace in the world!"

Peace with freedom. I smiled at the thought of somebody, not Howard Harvitz, painting that in red on the Soviet sign.

We drove on, I foreseeing my exit from the Soviet Union. I had made discreet inquiries from time to time and an Intourist girl in Leningrad had told me I had first to show my papers at the passport-control desk, turn in my rubles—a serious offense to walk off with any—and then check luggage; no inspection, she swore. And that was that. Unless, of course, the official at the passport desk found my name on a list and said I had to go to the customs office for a package. In that case—if nobody said so I wouldn't remind him—I would go get the books. I figured I wouldn't open the package, just tear off a bit of the wrapping, if they were wrapped, as though to make sure they were the books I expected, and then saunter away with the package under my arm. If they asked me to sign another five copies of a document in Russian I would write at the bottom: "It is understood that I can't speak or read Russian" and sign my name to that.

I had heard that a KGB man was stationed at the

ramp as one boarded a plane. He asked for your passport, checked the picture, threw you a stare through dark lenses, and if there was no serious lack of resemblance, tore out your expired visa, pocketed it, and let you embark.

In ten minutes you were aloft, seat belts fastened in three languages, watching the plane banking west. Maybe if I looked hard I might see in the distance Feliks Levitansky on the roof waving his red-white-and-blue socks on a bamboo pole. Then the plane leveled off, and we were above the clouds, flying westward. And that's what I would be doing for five or six hours unless the pilot received radio instructions to turn back; or maybe land in Czechoslovakia or East Germany, where two big-hatted detectives boarded the plane. By an act of imagination and will I made it some other passenger they were arresting. I got the plane into the air again and we flew on without incident until we touched down in London.

As the taxi approached the Moscow airport, fingering my ticket and gripping my suitcase handle, I wished for courage equal to Levitansky's when they discovered he was the author of a book of stories I had managed to sneak out and get published, and his trial and suffering began.

Levitansky's first story of the four in English was about an old father, a pensioner, who was not feeling well and wanted his son, with whom he had had continuous strong disagreements, and whom he hadn't seen in eight months, to know. He decided to pay him a short visit. Since the son had moved from his flat to a larger one and had not forwarded his address, the father went to call on him at work. The son was an official of some sort with an office in a new State building. The father had never been there although he knew where it was because a neighbor on a walk with him had pointed it out.

The pensioner sat in a chair in his son's large outer office, waiting for him to be free for a few minutes. "Yuri," he thought he would say, "all I want to tell you is that I'm not up to my usual self. My breath is short and I have pains in my chest. In fact, I'm not well. After all, we're father and son and you ought to know the state of my health, seeing it's not so good and your mother is dead."

The son's assistant secretary, a modern girl in a short tight skirt, said he was attending an important administrative conference.

"A conference is a conference," the father said. He wouldn't want to interfere with it and didn't mind waiting although he was still having nauseating twinges of pain.

The father waited patiently in the chair for several hours; and though he had a few times risen and urgently spoken to the assistant secretary, he was, by the end of the day, still unable to see his son. The girl, putting on her pink hat, advised the old man that the official had already left the building. He hadn't been able to see his father because he had unexpectedly been called away on an important State matter.

"Go home and he will telephone you in the morning."

"I have no telephone," said the old pensioner impatiently. "He knows that."

The assistant secretary; the private secretary, an older woman from the inside office; and later the caretaker of the building, all tried to persuade the father to go home, but he wouldn't leave.

The private secretary said her husband was expecting her and she could stay no longer. After a while the assistant secretary with the pink hat also left. The caretaker, a man with wet eyes and a ragged mustache, tried to persuade the old man to leave. "What sort of foolishness is it to wait all night in a pitch-dark building? You'll frighten yourself out of your wits, not to speak of other discomforts you're bound to suffer."

"No," said the sick father, "I will wait. When my son comes in tomorrow morning I'll tell him something he hasn't learned yet. I'll tell him what he does to me his children will do to him."

The caretaker departed. The old man was left alone waiting for his son to appear in the morning.

"I'll report him to the Party," he muttered.

The second story was about another old man, a widower of sixty-eight, who hoped to have matzos for Passover. Last year he had got his quota. They had been baked at the State bakery and sold in State stores; but this year the State bakeries were not permitted to bake them. The officials said the machines had broken down but who believed them.

The old man went to the rabbi, an older man with a

tormented beard, and asked him where he could get matzos. He was frightened that he mightn't have them this
year.

"So am I," confessed the old rabbi. He said he had
been told to tell his congregants to buy flour and bake them
at home. The State stores would sell them the flour.

"What good is that for me?" asked the widower. He
reminded the rabbi that he had no home to speak of, a
single small room with a one-burner electric stove. His
wife had died two years ago. His only living child, a married daughter, was with her husband in Birobijan. His
other relatives—the few who were left after the German
invasion—two female cousins his age—lived in Odessa; and
he himself, even if he could find an oven, did not know how
to bake matzos. And if he couldn't what should he do?

The rabbi then promised he would try to get the widower a kilo or two of matzos, and the old man, rejoicing,
blessed him.

He waited anxiously a month but the rabbi never mentioned the matzos. Maybe he had forgotten. After all he
was an old man burdened with worries and the widower
did not want to press him. However, Passover was coming
on wings, so he must do something. A week before the
Holy Days he hurried to the rabbi's flat and spoke to him
there.

"Rabbi," he begged, "you promised me a kilo or two
of matzos. What has happened to them?"

"I know I promised," said the rabbi, "but I'm no
longer sure to whom. It's easy to promise." He dabbed at

his face with a damp handkerchief. "I was warned one could be arrested on charges of profiteering in the production and sale of matzos. I was told it could happen even if I were to give them away for nothing. It's a new crime they've invented. Still, take them anyway. If they arrest me, I'm an old man, and how long can an old man live in Lubyanka? Not so long, thank God. Here, I'll give you a small pack but you must tell no one where you got the matzos."

"May the Lord eternally bless you, rabbi. As for dying in prison, rather let it happen to our enemies."

The rabbi went to his closet and got out a small pack of matzos, already wrapped and tied with knotted twine. When the widower offered in a whisper to pay him, at least the cost of the flour, the rabbi wouldn't hear of it. "God provides," he said, "although at times with difficulty." He said there was hardly enough for all who wanted matzos, so he must take what he got and be thankful.

"I will eat less," said the old man. "I will count mouthfuls. I will save the last matzo to look at and kiss if there isn't enough to last me. God will understand."

Overjoyed to have even a few matzos, he rode home on the trolley car and there met another Jew, a man with a withered hand. They conversed in Yiddish in low tones. The stranger had glanced at the almost square package, then at the widower, and had hoarsely whispered, "Matzos?" The widower, tears starting in his eyes, nodded. "With God's grace." "Where did you get them?" "God provides." "So if He provides let Him provide me," the

stranger brooded. "I'm not so lucky. I was hoping for a
package from relatives in Cleveland, America. They wrote
they would send me a large pack of the finest matzos but
when I inquire of the authorities they say no matzos have
arrived. You know when they will get here?" he muttered.
"After Passover by a month or two, and what good will
they be then?"

The widower nodded sadly. The stranger wiped his
eyes with his good hand and after a short while left the
trolley amid a number of people getting off. He had not
bothered to say goodbye, and neither had the widower, not
to remind him of his own good fortune. When the time
came for the old man to leave the trolley he glanced down
between his feet where he had placed the package of
matzos but nothing was there. His feet were there. The
old man felt harrowed, as though someone had ripped a
nail down his spine. He searched frantically throughout
that car, going a long way past his stop, querying every
passenger, the woman conductor, the motorman, but no
one had seen his matzos.

Then it occurred to him that the stranger with the
withered hand had stolen them.

The widower in his misery asked himself, would a Jew
have robbed another of his precious matzos? It didn't seem
possible. Still, who knows, he thought, what one will do to
get matzos if he has none.

As for me I haven't even a matzo to look at now. If I
could steal any, whether from Jew or Russian, I would steal
them. He thought he would even steal them from the old
rabbi.

The widower went home without his matzos and had none for Passover.

The third story, a tale called "Tallith," concerned a youth of seventeen, beardless but for some stray hairs on his chin, who had come from Kirov to the steps of the synagogue on Arkhipova Street in Moscow. He had brought with him a capacious prayer shawl, a white garment of luminous beauty which he offered for sale to a cluster of Jews of various sorts and sizes—curious, apprehensive, greedy at the sight of the shawl—for fifteen rubles. Most of them avoided the youth, particularly the older Jews, despite the fact that some of the more devout among them were worried about their prayer shawls, eroded on their shoulders after years of daily use, which they could not replace. "It's the informers among us who have put him up to this," they whispered among themselves, "so they will have someone to inform on."

Still, in spite of the warnings of their elders, several of the younger men examined the tallith and admired it. "Where did you get such a fine prayer shawl?" the youth was asked. "It was my father's who recently died," he said. "It was given to him by a rich Jew he had once befriended." "Then why don't you keep it for yourself, you're a Jew, aren't you?" "Yes," said the youth, not the least embarrassed, "but I am going to Bratsk as a komsomol volunteer and I need a few rubles to get married. Besides I'm a confirmed atheist."

One young man with fat unshaven cheeks, who ad-

mired the deeply white shawl, its white glowing in white-
ness, with its long silk fringes, whispered to the youth he
might consider buying it for five rubles. But he was over-
heard by the gabbai, the lay leader of the congregation,
who raised his cane and shouted at the whisperer, "Hooli-
gan, if you buy that shawl, beware it doesn't become your
shroud." The Jew with the unshaven cheeks retreated.

"Don't strike him," cried the frightened rabbi, who
had come out of the synagogue and saw the gabbai, with
his cane upraised. He urged the congregants to begin
prayers at once. To the youth he said, "Please go away
from here, we are burdened with enough troubles as it is.
It is forbidden for anyone to sell religious articles. Do you
want us to be accused of criminal economic activity? Do
you want the doors of the shul to be closed forever? So do
us and yourself a mitzvah and go away."

The congregants moved inside. The youth was left
standing alone on the steps; but then the gabbai came out
of the door, a man with a deformed spine and a wad of
cotton stuck in his leaking ear.

"Look here," he said. "I know you stole it. Still, after
all is said and done, a tallith is a tallith and God asks no
questions of His worshippers. I offer eight rubles for it,
take it or leave it. Talk fast before the services end and the
others come out."

"Make it ten and it's yours," said the youth.

The gabbai gazed at him shrewdly. "Eight is all I
have but wait here and I'll borrow two rubles from my
brother-in-law."

The youth waited patiently. Dusk was thickening. In a few minutes a black car drove up, stopped in front of the synagogue, and two policemen got out. The youth realized at once that the gabbai had informed on him. Not knowing what else to do he hastily draped the prayer shawl over his head and began loudly to pray. He prayed a passionate kaddish. The police hesitated to approach him while he was praying, and they stood at the bottom of the steps waiting for him to be done. The congregants came out and could not believe their ears. No one imagined the youth could pray so fervently. What moved them was the tone, the wail and passion of a man truly praying. Perhaps his father had indeed recently died. All listened attentively, and many wished he would pray forever, for they knew that when he stopped he would be seized and thrown into prison.

It has grown dark. A moon hovers behind murky clouds over the synagogue steeple. The youth's voice is heard in prayer. The congregants are huddled in the dark street, listening. Both police agents are still there, although they cannot be seen. Neither can the youth. All that can be seen is the white shawl luminously praying.

The last of the four stories translated by Irina Filipovna was about a writer of mixed parentage, a Russian father and Jewish mother, who had secretly been writing stories for years. He had from a young age wanted to write but had at first not had the courage to—it seemed like such a merciless undertaking—so he had gone into translation instead; and then when he had, one day, started to write seriously and exultantly, after a while he found to his surprise that many of his stories, about half, were about Jews.

For a half-Jew that's a reasonable proportion, he thought. The others were about Russians who sometimes resembled members of his father's family. "It's good to have such different sources for ideas," he told his wife. "This way I can cover a varied range of experiences in life."

After several years of work he had submitted a selection of his stories to a trusted friend of university days, Viktor Zverkov, an editor of the Progress Publishing House; and the writer appeared at his office one morning after receiving a hastily scribbled cryptic note from his friend, to discuss his work with him. Zverkov, a troubled man to begin with—he told everyone his wife did not respect him —jumped up from his chair and turned the key in the door, his ear pressed a minute at the crack. He then went quickly to his desk and withdrew the manuscript from a drawer he first had to unlock with a key he kept in his pocket. He was a heavy-set man with a flushed complexion, stained teeth, and a hoarse voice; and he handled the writer's manuscript with unease, as though it might leap up and wound him in the face.

"Please, Tolya," he whispered breathily, bringing his head close to the writer's, "you must take these dreadful stories away at once."

"What's the matter with you? Why are you shaking so?"

"Don't pretend to be so naïve. You know why I am disturbed. I am frankly amazed that you are submitting such unorthodox material for publication. My opinion as an editor is that they are of doubtful literary merit—I won't say devoid of it, Tolya, I want to be honest—but as stories they are a frightful affront to our society. I can't understand why you should take it on yourself to write about Jews. What do you know about them? Your culture is not the least Jewish, it's Soviet Russian. The whole business smacks of hypocrisy and you may be accused of anti-Semitism."

He got up to shut the window and peered into a closet before sitting down.

"Are you out of your mind, Viktor? My stories are in no sense anti-Semitic. One would have to read them standing on his head to make that judgment."

"There can be only one logical interpretation," the editor argued. "According to my most lenient analysis, which is favorable to you as a person of let's call it decent intent, the stories fly in the face of socialist realism and reveal a dangerous inclination—perhaps even a stronger word should be used—to anti-Soviet sentiment. Maybe you're not entirely aware of this—I know how a story can pull a writer by the nose. As an editor I have to be sensitive to such things. I know, Tolya, from our conversations that you are a sincere believer in our socialism; I won't accuse you of being defamatory to the Soviet system, but others may. In fact, I know they will. If one of the editors of *Oktyabr* were to read your stories, believe me, your career would explode in a mess. You seem not to have a normal awareness of what self-preservation is, and what's appallingly worse, you're not above entangling innocent bystanders in your fate. If these stories were mine, I assure you I would never have brought them to you. I urge you to destroy them at once, before they destroy you."

He drank thirstily from a glass of water on his desk.

"That's the last thing I would do," answered the writer in anger. "These stories, if not in tone or subject matter, are written in the spirit of our early Soviet writers—the joyous spirits of the years just after the Revolution."

"I think you know what happened to many of those 'joyous spirits.'"

The writer for a moment stared at him. "Well, then, what of the stories that are not about the experience of Jews? Some are pieces about homely aspects of Russian life; for instance the one about the pensioner father and his invisible son. What I hoped is that you might personally recommend one or two such stories to *Novy Mir* or *Yunost*. They are innocuous sketches and well written."

"Not the one of the two prostitutes," said the editor. "That contains hidden social criticism and is adversely naturalistic."

"A prostitute lives a social life."

"That may be but I can't recommend it for publication. I must advise you, Tolya, if you expect to receive further commissions for translations from us, you must immediately rid yourself of this whole manuscript so as to avoid the possibility of serious consequences both to yourself and family, and to this publishing house that has employed you so faithfully and generously in the past."

"Since you didn't write the stories yourself, you needn't be afraid, Viktor Alexandrovich," the writer said coldly.

"I am not a coward, if that's what you're hinting, Anatoly Borisovich, but if a wild locomotive is running loose on the rails, I know which way to jump."

The writer hastily gathered up his manuscript, stuffed the papers into his leather case, and returned home by bus. His wife was still away at work. He took out the stories, and after reading through one, burned it, page by page, in the kitchen sink.

His nine-year-old son, returning from school, said, "Papa, what are you burning in the sink? That's no place for a fire."

"I am burning my integrity," said the writer. Then he said, "My talent. My heritage."

The Letter

———

A T the gate stands Teddy holding his letter.

On Sunday afternoons Newman sat with his father on
a white bench in the open ward. The son had brought a
pineapple tart but the old man wouldn't eat it.

Twice during the two and a half hours he spent in the
ward with his father, Newman said, "Do you want me to
come back next Sunday or don't you? Do you want to have
next Sunday off?"

The old man said nothing. Nothing meant yes or it meant no. If you pressed him to say which he wept.

"All right, I'll see you next Sunday. But if you want a week off sometime, let me know. I want a Sunday off myself."

His father said nothing. Then his mouth moved and after a while he said, "Your mother didn't talk to me like that. She didn't like to leave any dead chickens in the bathtub. When is she coming to see me here?"

"Pa, she's been dead since before you got sick and tried to take your life. Try to keep that in your memory."

"Don't ask me to believe that one," his father said, and Newman got up to go to the station where he took the Long Island Rail Road train to New York City.

He said, "Get better, Pa," when he left, and his father answered, "Don't tell me that. I am better."

Sundays after he left his father in Ward 12 of Building B and walked across the hospital grounds, that spring and dry summer, at the arched iron-barred gate between brick posts under a towering oak that shadowed the raw red brick wall, he met Teddy standing there with his letter in his hand. Newman could have got out through the main entrance of Building B of the hospital complex, but this way to the railroad station was shorter. The gate was open to visitors on Sundays only.

Teddy was a stout soft man in loose gray institutional clothes and canvas slippers. He was fifty or more and maybe so was his letter. He held it as he always held it, as though he had held it always, a thick squarish finger-soiled blue envelope with unsealed flap. Inside were four sheets of cream paper with nothing written on them. After he had looked at the paper the first time, Newman had handed the envelope back to Teddy, and the green-uniformed guard had let him out of the gate. Sometimes there were other patients standing by the gate who wanted to walk out with Newman but the guard said they couldn't.

"What about mailing my letter," Teddy said on Sundays.

He handed Newman the finger-smudged envelope. It was easier to take, then hand back, than to refuse to take it.

The mailbox hung on a short cement pole just outside the iron gate on the other side of the road, a few feet from the oak tree. Teddy would throw a right jab in its direction as though at the mailbox through the gate. Once it had been painted red and was now painted blue. There was also a mailbox in the doctor's office in each ward, Newman had reminded him, but Teddy said he didn't want the doctor reading his letter.

"You bring it to the office and so they read it."

"That's his job," Newman answered.

"Not on my head," said Teddy. "Why don't you mail it? It won't do you any good if you don't."

"There's nothing in it to mail."

"That's what you say."

His heavy head was set on a short sunburned neck, the coarse grizzled hair cropped an inch from the skull. One of his eyes was a fleshy gray, the other was walleyed.

He stared beyond Newman when he talked to him, sometimes through his shoulder. And Newman noticed he never so much as glanced at the blue envelope when it was momentarily out of his hand, when Newman was holding it. Once in a while he pointed a short finger at something but said nothing. When he said nothing he rose a little on the balls of his toes. The guard did not interfere when Teddy handed Newman the letter every Sunday.

Newman gave it back.

"It's your mistake," said Teddy. Then he said, "I got my walking privileges. I'm almost sane. I fought in Guadalcanal."

Newman said he knew that.

"Where did you fight?"

"Nowhere yet."

"Why don't you mail my letter out?"

"It's for your own good the doctor reads it."

"That's a hot one." Teddy stared at the mailbox through Newman's shoulder.

"The letter isn't addressed to anybody and there's no stamp on it."

"Put one on. They won't let me buy one three or three ones."

"It's eight cents now. I'll put one on if you address the envelope."

"Not me," said Teddy.

Newman no longer asked why.

"It's not that kind of a letter."

He asked what kind it was.

"Blue with white paper inside of it."

"Saying what?"

"Shame on you," said Teddy.

Newman left on the four o'clock train. The ride home was not so bad as the ride there, though Sundays were murderous.

Teddy holds his letter.

"No luck?"

"No luck," said Newman.

"It's off your noodle."

He handed the envelope to Newman anyway and after a while Newman gave it back.

Teddy stared at his shoulder.

Ralph holds the finger-soiled blue envelope.

On Sunday a tall lean grim old man, clean-shaven, faded-eyed, wearing a worn-thin World War I overseas cap on his yellowed white head, stood at the gate with Teddy. He looked eighty.

The guard in the green uniform told him to step back, he was blocking the gate.

"Step back, Ralph, you're in the way of the gate."

"Why don't you stick it in the box on your way out?" Ralph asked in a gravelly old man's voice, handing the letter to Newman.

Newman wouldn't take it. "Who are you?"

Teddy and Ralph said nothing.

"It's his father," the guard at the gate said.

"Whose?"

"Teddy."

"My God," said Newman. "Are they both in here?"

"That's right," said the guard.

"Was he just admitted or has he been here all the while?"

"He just got his walking privileges returned again. They were revoked about a year."

"I got them back after five years," Ralph said.

"One year."

"Five."

"It's astonishing anyway," Newman said. "Neither one of you resembles the other."

"Who do you resemble?" asked Ralph.

Newman couldn't say.

"What war were you in?" Ralph asked.

"No war at all."

"That settles your pickle. Why don't you mail my letter?"

Teddy stood by sullenly. He rose on his toes and threw a short right and left at the mailbox.

"I thought it was Teddy's letter."

"He told me to mail it for him. He fought at Iwo Jima. We fought two wars. I fought in the Marne and the Argonne Forest. I had both my lungs gassed with mustard gas. The wind changed and the Huns were gassed. That's not all that were."

"Tough turd," said Teddy.

"Mail it anyway for the poor kid," said Ralph. His tall body trembled. He was an angular man with deep-set bluish eyes and craggy features that looked as though they had been hacked out of a tree.

"I told your son I would if he wrote something on the paper," Newman said.

"What do you want it to say?"

"Anything he wants it to. Isn't there somebody he wants to communicate with? If he doesn't want to write it he could tell me what to say and I'll write it out."

"Tough turd," said Teddy.

"He wants to communicate to me," said Ralph.

"It's not a bad idea," Newman said. "Why doesn't he write a few words to you? Or you could write a few words to him."

"A Bronx cheer on you."

"It's my letter," Teddy said.

"I don't care who writes it," said Newman. "I could write a message for you wishing him luck. I could say you hope he gets out of here soon."

"A Bronx cheer to that."

"Not in my letter," Teddy said.

"Not in mine either," said Ralph grimly. "Why don't you mail it like it is? I bet you're afraid to."

"No I'm not."

"I'll bet you are."

"No I'm not."

"I have my bets going."

"There's nothing to mail. There's nothing in the letter. It's a blank."

"What makes you think so?" asked Ralph. "There's a whole letter in there. Plenty of news."

"I'd better be going," Newman said, "or I'll miss my train."

The guard opened the gate to let him out. Then he shut the gate.

Teddy turned away and stared over the oak tree into the summer sun with his gray eye and his walleyed one.

Ralph trembled at the gate.

"Who do you come here to see on Sundays?" he called to Newman.

"My father."

"What war was he in?"

"The war in his head."

"Has he got his walking privileges?"

"No, they won't give him any."

"What I mean, he's crazy?"

"That's right," said Newman, walking away.

"So are you," said Ralph. "Why don't you come back in here and hang around with the rest of us?"

In Retirement

H E had lately taken to studying his old Greek grammar of fifty years ago. He read in Bulfinch and wanted to re-read the *Odyssey* in Greek. His life had changed. He slept less these days and in the morning got up to stare at the sky over Gramercy Park. He watched the clouds until they took on shapes he could reflect on. He liked strange, haunted vessels and he liked to watch mythological birds and animals. He had noticed that if he contemplated these forms in the clouds, could keep his mind on them for a while, there might be a diminution of his morning depression. Dr. Morris was sixty-six, a physician, retired for two years. He had shut down his practice in Queens and moved to Manhattan. He had retired himself after a heart attack, not too serious but serious enough. It was his first attack and he hoped his last, though in the end he hoped to go quickly. His wife was dead and his daughter lived in Scotland. He wrote her twice a month and heard from her twice a month. And though he had a few friends he visited, and kept up with medical journals, and liked museums and theater, generally he contended with loneliness. And he was concerned about the future; the future was old age possessed.

After a light breakfast he would dress warmly and go out for a walk around the Square. That was the easy part of the walk. He took this walk even when it was very cold, or nasty rainy, or had snowed several inches and he had to proceed very slowly. After the Square he crossed the street and went down Irving Place, a tall figure with a cape and cane, and picked up his *Times*. If the weather was not too bad he continued on to Fourteenth Street, around to Park Avenue South, up Park and along East Twentieth back to the narrow, tall, white stone apartment building he lived in. Rarely, lately, had he gone in another direction, though when on the long walk, he stopped at least once on the way, perhaps in front of a mid-block store, perhaps at a street corner, and asked himself where else he might go. This was the difficult part of the walk. What was difficult was that it made no difference where he went. He now wished he had not retired. He had become more conscious of his age since his retirement, although sixty-six was not eighty. Still it was old. He experienced moments of anguish.

One morning after his rectangular long walk in the rain, Dr. Morris found a letter on the rubber mat under the line of mailboxes in the lobby. It was a narrow, deep lobby with false green marble columns and several bulky chairs where few people ever sat. Dr. Morris had seen a young woman with long hair, in a white raincoat and maroon shoulder bag, carrying a cellophane bubble umbrella, hurry down the vestibule steps and leave the house as he was about to enter. In fact he held the door open for her and got a breath of her bold perfume. He did not remember seeing her before and felt a momentary confusion as to who she might be. He later imagined her taking the letter out of her box, reading it hastily, then stuffing it into the maroon cloth purse she carried over her shoulder; but she had stuffed in the envelope and not the letter. That had fallen to the floor. He imagined this as he bent to retrieve it. It was a folded sheet of heavy white writing paper, written on in black in a masculine hand. The doctor unfolded and glanced at it without making out the salutation or any of its contents. He would have to put on his reading glasses, and he thought Flaherty, the doorman and elevator man, might see him if the elevator should suddenly descend. Of course Flaherty might think the doctor was reading his own mail, except that he never read it, such as it was, in the lobby. He did not want the man thinking he was reading someone else's letter. He also thought of handing him the letter and describing the young woman who had dropped it. Perhaps he could return it to her? But for some reason not at once clear to him the doctor slipped it into his pocket to take upstairs to read. His arm began to tremble and he felt his heart racing at a rate that bothered him.

After the doctor had got his own mail out of the box —nothing more than the few circulars he held in his hand— Flaherty took him up to the fifteenth floor. Flaherty spelled the night man at 8 a.m. and was himself relieved at 4 p.m. He was a slender man of sixty with sparse white hair on his half-bald head, who had lost part of his jaw under the left ear after two bone operations. He would be out for a few months; then return, the lower part of the left side of his face caved in; still it was not a bad face to look at. Although the doorman never spoke about his ailment, the doctor knew he was not done with cancer of the jaw, but of course he kept this to himself; and he sensed when the man was concealing pain.

This morning, though preoccupied, he asked, "How is it going, Mr. Flaherty?"

"Not too tough."

"Not a bad day." He said this, thinking not of the rain but of the letter in his pocket.

"Fine and dandy," Flaherty quipped. On the whole he moved and talked animatedly and was careful to align the elevator with the floor before letting passengers off. Sometimes the doctor wished he could say more to him than he did; but not this morning.

He stood by the large double window of his living room overlooking the Square, in the dull rainy-day February light, in pleasurable excitement reading the letter he had found, the kind he had anticipated it might be. It was a letter written by a father to his daughter, addressed to "Dear Evelyn." What it expressed after an irresolute start was the father's dissatisfaction with his daughter's way of life. And it ended with an exhortatory paragraph of advice: "You have slept around long enough. I don't understand what you get out of that type of behavior any more. I think you have tried everything there is to try. You claim you are a serious person but let men use you for what they can get. There is no true payoff to you unless it is very temporary, and the real payoff to them is that they have got themselves an easy lay. I know how they think about this and how they talk about it in the lavatory the next day. Now I want to urge you once and for all that you ought to be more serious about your life. You have experimented long enough. I honestly and sincerely and urgently advise you to look around for a man of steady habits and good character who will marry you and treat you like the person I believe you want to be. I don't want to think of you any more as a drifting semi-prostitute. Please follow this advice, the age of twenty-nine is no longer sixteen." The letter was signed, "Your Father," and under his signature, another sentence, in neat small handwriting, was appended: "Your sex life fills me full of fear." "Mother."

The doctor put the letter away in a drawer. His excitement had left him and he felt ashamed of having read it. He was sympathetic to the father and at the same time

sympathetic to the young woman, though perhaps less so
to her. After a while he tried to study his Greek grammar
but could not concentrate. The letter remained in his mind
like a billboard sign as he was reading *The Times* and he
was conscious of it throughout the day, as though it had
aroused in him some sort of expectation he could not define. Sentences from it would replay themselves in his
thoughts. He reveried the young woman as he had imagined
her after reading what the father had written, and as the
woman—was she Evelyn?—he had seen coming out of the
house. He could not be certain the letter was hers. Perhaps
it was not; still he thought of the letter as though belonging
to her, the woman he had held the door for, whose perfume
still lingered in his senses. That night thoughts of her kept
him from falling asleep. "I'm too old for this nonsense." He
got up to read and was able to concentrate, but when his
head lay once more on the pillow, a long freight train of
thoughts of her rumbled by drawn by a black locomotive.
He pictured Evelyn, the drifting semi-prostitute, in bed
with various lovers, engaged in various acts of sex. Once
she lay alone, erotically naked in bed, her maroon cloth
purse drawn close to her nude body. He also thought of
her as an ordinary girl with many fewer lovers than her
father seemed to think. This was probably closer to the
truth. He wondered if he could be useful to her in some
way. He then felt a fright he could not explain but managed to dispel it by promising himself to burn the letter in
the morning. The freight train, with its many cars, disappeared in the foggy distance. When the doctor awoke at

10 a.m. on a sunny winter's morning, there was no sense, light or heavy, of his usual depression.

But he did not burn the letter. He reread it several times during the day, each time returning it to his desk drawer and locking it there. Then he unlocked the drawer to read it again. As the day passed he was aware of an unappeased insistent hunger in himself. He recalled memories, experienced intense longing, desires he had not felt in years. The doctor was worried, alarmed by this change in him, this disturbance. He tried to blot the letter out of his mind but could not. Yet he would still not burn it, as though if he did he had shut the door on certain possibilities in his life, other ways to go, whatever that might mean. He was astonished—even thought of it as affronted, that this should be happening to him at his age. He had seen it in others, in former patients, but had not expected it in himself. The hunger he felt, a hunger for pleasure, disruption of habit, renewal of feeling, yet a fear of it, continued to grow in him like a dead tree come to life and spreading its branches. He felt as though he were hungry for exotic experience, which, if he were to have it, might make him forever ravenously hungry. He did not want that to happen to him. He recalled mythological figures: Sisyphus, Midas, who for one reason or another had been eternally cursed. He thought of Tithonus, his youth gone, become a grasshopper living forever. The doctor felt he was caught in an overwhelming emotion, a fearful dark wind.

When Flaherty left for the day at 4 p.m. and Silvio, who had tight curly black hair, was on duty, Dr. Morris came down and sat in the lobby, pretending to read his newspaper. As soon as the elevator ascended he approached the letter boxes and quickly scanned the name plates for an Evelyn, whoever she might be. He found no Evelyns though there was an E. Gordon and an E. Cummings. He suspected one of them might be she. He knew that single women often preferred not to reveal their first names in order to keep cranks at a distance, conceal themselves from potential annoyers. He casually asked Silvio if Miss Gordon or Miss Cummings was named Evelyn, but Silvio said he didn't know although probably Mr. Flaherty would because he distributed the mail. "Too many peoples in this house," Silvio shrugged. Embarrassed, the doctor remarked he was just curious, a lame remark but all he could think of. He went out for an aimless short walk and when he returned said nothing more to Silvio. They rode silently up in the elevator, the doctor standing tall, almost stiff. That night he again slept badly. When he fell deeply asleep a moment his dreams were erotic. He woke with desire mixed with repulsion and lay quietly mourning himself. He felt powerless to be other than he was.

He was up before five and though he tried to kill time was uselessly in the lobby before seven. He felt he must find out, settle in his mind, who she was. In the lobby, Richard, the night man who had brought him down, returned to a pornographic paperback he was reading; the mail, as Dr. Morris knew, hadn't come. He knew it would not arrive until shortly after eight but hadn't the patience to wait in his apartment. So he left the building, bought *The Times* on Irving Place, continued on his walk, and because it was a pleasant morning, not too cold, sat on a bench in Union Square Park. He stared at the paper but could not read it. He watched some sparrows pecking at dead grass. He was an old man, true enough; but he had lived long enough to know that age often meant little in man-woman relationships. He was still vigorous and bodies are bodies. He was back in the lobby at eight-thirty, an act of great restraint. Flaherty had received the mail sack and was alphabetizing the first-class letters on a long large table before distributing them into the boxes. He did not look well today. He moved slowly. His misshapen face was gray; the mouth slack, one heard his breathing; his eyes harbored pain.

"Nothin for you yet," he said to the doctor without looking up.

"I'll wait this morning," said Dr. Morris. "I ought to be hearing from my daughter."

"Nothin yet but you might hit the lucky number in this last bundle." He removed the string.

As he was alphabetizing the last bundle of letters the elevator buzzed and Flaherty had to go up for a call.

The doctor pretended to be absorbed in his *Times*. When he heard the elevator door shut he sat momentarily still, then went to the table and hastily rifled through the C pile of letters. E. Cummings was Ernest Cummings. He shuffled through the G's, watching the metal arrow as it showed the elevator beginning to descend. In the G pile there were two letters addressed to Evelyn Gordon. One was from her mother. The other, also handwritten, was from a Lee Bradley. Almost against the will the doctor removed this letter and slipped it into his suit pocket. His body was sweaty hot. This is an aberration, he thought. He was sitting in the chair turning the page of his newspaper when the elevator door opened.

"Nothin at all for you," Flaherty said after a moment.

"Thank you," said Dr. Morris. "I think I'll go up now."

In his apartment the doctor, conscious of his whisperous breathing, placed the letter on the kitchen table and sat looking at it, waiting for a tea kettle of water to boil. The kettle whistled as it boiled but still he sat with the unopened letter before him. For a while he sat there with dulled thoughts. Soon he fantasied what the letter said. He fantasied Lee Bradley describing the sexual pleasure he had had with Evelyn Gordon, and telling her what else they might try. He fantasied the lovers' acts they engaged in. Then though he audibly told himself not to, he steamed open the flap of the envelope. His hands trembled as he held the letter. He had to place it down flat on the table so he could read it. His heart beat heavily in anticipation of what he might read. But to his surprise the letter was a bore, an egoistic account of some stupid business deal this Bradley was concocting. Only the last sentences came surprisingly to life. "Be in your bed when I get there tonight. Be wearing only your white panties. I don't like to waste time once we are together." The doctor didn't know whom he was more disgusted with, this fool or him-

self. In truth, himself. Slipping the sheet of paper into the
envelope, he resealed it with a thin layer of paste he had
rubbed carefully on the flap with his fingertip. Later in the
day he tucked the letter into his inside pocket and pressed
the elevator button for Silvio. The doctor left the building
and soon returned with a copy of the afternoon *Post* he
seemed to be involved with until Silvio had to take up two
women who had come into the lobby; then the doctor
thrust the letter into Evelyn Gordon's box and went out
for a breath of air.

He was sitting near the table in the lobby when the
young woman he had held the door open for came in
shortly after 6 p.m. He was aware of her cool perfume almost at once. Silvio was not around at that moment; he
had gone down to the basement to eat a sandwich. She
inserted a small key into Evelyn Gordon's mailbox and
stood before the open box, smoking, as she read Bradley's
letter. She was wearing a light-blue pants suit with a brown
knit sweater-coat. Her tail of black hair was tied with a
brown silk scarf. Her face, though a little heavy, was
pretty, her intense eyes blue, the lids lightly eye-shadowed.
Her body, he thought, was finely proportioned. She had
not noticed him but he was more than half in love with
her.

He observed her many mornings. He would come
down later now, at nine, and spend some time going
through the medical circulars he had got out of his box,
sitting on a thronelike wooden chair near a tall unlit lamp
in the rear of the lobby. He would watch people as they

left for work or shopping in the morning. Evelyn appeared at about half-past nine and stood smoking in front of her box, absorbed in the morning's mail. When spring came she wore brightly colored skirts with pastel blouses, or light slim pants suits. Sometimes she wore very short minidresses. Her figure was exquisite. She received many letters and read most of them with apparent pleasure, some with what seemed suppressed excitement. A few she gave short shrift to, scanned these quickly and stuffed them into her bag. He imagined they were from her father, or mother. He thought that most of her letters came from lovers, past and present, and he felt a curious anguish that there was none from him in her box. He would write to her.

He thought it through carefully. Some women needed an older man; it stabilized their lives. Sometimes a difference of as many as thirty or even thirty-five years offered no serious disadvantages, granted differences in metabolism, energy. There would of course be less sex, but there would be sex. His would go on for a long time; he knew that from the experience of friends and former patients, not to speak of medical literature. A younger woman inspired an older man to remain virile. And despite the heart incident his health was good, in some ways better than before. A girl like Evelyn, probably at odds with herself, could benefit from a steadying relationship with an older man, someone who would respect and love her and help her to respect and love herself more than she perhaps presently did; who would demand less from her in certain ways than some young men awash in their egoism; who would awake in her a stronger sense of well-being, and if things went quite well, perhaps even love for one particular man.

"I am a retired physician, a widower," he wrote to Evelyn Gordon. "I write to you with some hesitation and circumspection, although needless to say with high regard, because I am old enough to be your father. I have observed you often in this building and sometimes as we passed by each other in nearby streets, and I have grown to admire you deeply. I wonder if you will permit me to make your acquaintance? I wonder if you would care to have dinner with me and perhaps enjoy a film or performance of a play? My intentions, as used to be said when I was a young man, are 'ancient and honorable.' I do not think my company will disappoint you. If you are so inclined—so kind, certainly—to consider this request tolerantly, I will be obliged if you will place a note to that effect in my mailbox. I am respectfully yours, Simon Morris, M.D."

He did not go down to mail his letter at once. He thought he would keep it to the last moment. Then he had a fright about it that woke him out of momentary deep sleep. He dreamed he had written and sealed the letter and then remembered he had appended another sentence: "Be wearing only your white panties." When he woke he wanted to tear open the envelope to see whether he had included Bradley's remark. But when he was thoroughly waked up, in his senses, he knew he had not. He bathed and shaved early and for a while observed the cloud formations out the window. None of them interested him.

At close to nine Dr. Morris descended to the lobby. He would wait till Flaherty answered a buzz, and when he was gone, drop his letter into her box; but Flaherty that morning seemed to have no calls to answer. The doctor had forgotten it was Saturday. He did not know it was till he got his *Times* and sat with it in the lobby, pretending to be waiting for the mail delivery. The mail sack arrived late on Saturdays. At last he heard a prolonged buzz, and Flaherty, who had been on his knees polishing the brass door knob, got up on one foot, then rose on both legs and walked slowly to the elevator. His asymmetric face was gray. Shortly before ten o'clock the doctor slipped his letter into Evelyn Gordon's mailbox. He decided to withdraw to his apartment but then thought he would rather wait where he usually waited while she collected her mail. She had never noticed him there.

The mail sack was dropped in the vestibule at ten-after, and Flaherty alphabetized the first bundle before he had to respond to another call. The doctor read his paper in the dark rear of the lobby because he was really not reading it. He was anticipating Evelyn's coming. He had on a new green suit, blue striped shirt, and a pink tie. He was wearing a new hat. He waited in anticipation and love.

When the elevator door opened Evelyn walked out in an elegant slit black skirt, sandals, her hair tied with a red scarf. A sharp-featured man with puffed sideburns and carefully combed medium-long hair, in a turn-of-the-century haircut, followed her out of the elevator. He was shorter than she by half a head. Flaherty handed her two letters, which she dropped into the black patent-leather pouch she was carrying. The doctor thought—hoped—she would walk past the mailboxes without stopping; but she saw the white of his letter through the slot and stopped to remove it. She tore open the envelope, pulled out the single sheet of handwritten paper, and read it with immediate intense concentration. The doctor raised his newspaper to his eyes, though he could still watch over the top of it. He watched in fear.

How mad I was not to anticipate she might come down with a man.

When she had finished reading the letter, she handed it to her companion—possibly Bradley—who read it, grinned broadly, and said something inaudible when he handed it back to her.

Evelyn Gordon quietly ripped the letter into small bits, and turning, flung the pieces in the doctor's direction. The fragments came at him like a blast of wind-driven snow. He thought he would sit forever on his wooden throne in the swirling snow.

The old doctor sat lifelessly in his chair, the floor around him littered with his torn-up letter.

Flaherty swept it up with his little broom into a metal container. He handed the doctor a thin envelope stamped with foreign stamps.

"Here's a letter from your daughter just came."

The doctor, trying to stand without moving, pressed the bridge of his nose. He wiped his eyes with his fingers.

"There's no setting old age aside," he said after a while.

"Not in some ways," said Flaherty.

"Or death."

"It moves up on you."

The doctor tried to say something kind to him but could not.

Flaherty took him up to the fifteenth floor in his elevator.

Rembrandt's Hat

—

RUBIN, in careless white cloth hat or visorless soft round cap, however one described it, wandered with un-expressed or inexpressive thoughts up the stairs from his studio in the basement of the New York art school, where he made his sculpture, to a workshop on the second floor, where he taught it. Arkin, the art historian, a hypertensive impulsive bachelor of thirty-four—a man often swept by strong feeling, he thought—about a dozen years younger than the sculptor, observed him through his open office door, wearing the cap among a crowd of art students and teachers he wandered amid along the hall during a change of classes. In his white hat he stands out and apart, the art historian thought. It illumines a lonely inexpressiveness arrived at after years of experience. Though it was not entirely apt he imagined a lean white animal—hind, stag, goat?—staring steadfastly, but despondently, through trees of a dense wood. Their gazes momentarily interlocked and parted. Rubin hurried to his workshop class.

Arkin was friendly with Rubin though they were not really friends. Not his fault, he felt; the sculptor was a very private person. When they talked he listened looking away, as though guarding his impressions. Attentive, apparently, he seemed to be thinking of something else, his sad life no doubt, if saddened eyes, a faded green mistakable for gray, necessarily denote sad life. Once in a while he uttered an opinion, usually a flat statement about the nature of life, or art, never much about himself; and he said absolutely nothing about his work. "Are you working, Rubin?" Arkin was reduced to. "Of course I'm working." "What are you doing if I may ask?" "I have a thing going."

There Arkin let it lie.

Once, in the faculty cafeteria, listening to the art historian discourse at long length on the work of Jackson Pollock, the sculptor's anger had momentarily flared.

"The world of art ain't necessarily in your eyes."

"I have to believe that what I see is there," Arkin had politely but stiffly responded.

"Have you ever painted?" asked Rubin.

"Painting is my life," retorted Arkin.

Rubin, with dignity, reverted to silence. That evening, leaving the building, they tipped hats to each other over small smiles.

In recent years, after his wife left him and costume and headdress became a mode among students, Rubin had taken to wearing various odd hats from time to time, and this white one was the newest, resembling Nehru's Congress Party cap, but rounded, a cross between a cantor's hat and a bloated yarmulke; or perhaps like a French judge's in Rouault, or a working doctor's in a Daumier print. Rubin wore it like a crown. Maybe it kept his head warm under the cold skylight of his large studio.

When the sculptor afterwards again passed along the crowded hall on his way down to the studio that day he had first appeared in his white cap, Arkin, who had been reading a fascinating article on Giacometti, put it down and went quickly into the hall. He was in an ebullient mood he could not explain to himself and told Rubin he very much admired his hat.

"I'll tell you why I like it so much. It looks like Rembrandt's hat that he wears in one of the middle-aged self-portraits, the really profound ones, I think the one in the Rijksmuseum in Amsterdam. May it bring you the best of luck."

Rubin, who had for a moment looked as though he were struggling to say something extraordinary, fixed Arkin in a strong stare and hurried downstairs. That ended the incident, though not the art historian's pleasure in his observation.

Arkin later remembered that when he had come to the

art school via an assistant curator's job in a museum in St. Louis seven years ago, Rubin had been working in wood; he now welded triangular pieces of scrap iron to construct his sculptures. Working at one time with a hatchet, later a modified small meat cleaver, he had reshaped driftwood pieces, out of which he had created some arresting forms. Dr. Levis, the director of the art school, had talked the sculptor into giving an exhibition of his altered driftwood objects in one of the downtown galleries near where Levis lived. Arkin, in his first term at the school, had gone on the subway to see the show one brisk winter's day. This man is an original, he thought, maybe his work will be too. Rubin had refused a gallery vernissage and on the opening day the place was nearly deserted. The sculptor, as though escaping his hacked forms, had retreated into a storage room at the rear of the gallery and stayed there looking at pictures. Arkin, after reflecting whether he ought to, sought him out to say hello, but seeing Rubin seated on a crate with his back to him, examining a folio of somebody's prints without once turning to see who had come into the room, he silently shut the door and departed. Although in time two notices of the show appeared, one dreadful, the other mildly favorable, the sculptor seemed unhappy about exhibiting his work and after that hadn't for years. Nor had there been any sales. Recently, when Arkin had casually suggested it might be a good idea to show what he was doing with his welded iron triangles, Rubin, after a wildly inexpressive moment, had answered, "Don't bother playing around with that idea."

The day after the art historian's remarks in the hall
to Rubin about his white cap, it disappeared from sight—
gone totally; for a while he wore on his head nothing but
his heavy reddish hair. And a week or two later, though
he could momentarily not believe it, it seemed to Arkin
that the sculptor was actively avoiding him. He guessed
the man was no longer using the staircase to the right
of his office but was coming up from the basement on the
other side of the building, where his corner workshop room
was anyway, so he wouldn't have to pass Arkin's open door.
When he was certain of this Arkin felt at first uneasy, then
experienced intermittent moments of strong anger.

Have I offended him in some way? the art historian
asked himself. If so, what did I say that's so offensive? All
I did was remark on the hat in one of Rembrandt's self-
portraits and say it looked like the cap he was wearing
that day. How can that be so offensive?

He then thought: no offense where none's intended.
All I had was good will to him. He's shy and might have
been embarrassed in some way—maybe my exuberant voice
in the presence of students—if that's so, it's no fault of
mine. And if that's not it, I don't know what's the matter
other than his nature. Maybe he hasn't been feeling well,
or it's some momentary mishigas—nowadays there are more
ways of insult without meaning to than ever before—so
why raise up a sweat over it? I'll wait it out.

But as weeks, then a couple of months went by and
Rubin continued to shun the art historian—he saw the
sculptor only at faculty meetings when Rubin attended

them; and once in a while glimpsed him going up or down the left staircase; or sitting in the Fine Arts secretary's office poring over long inventory lists of supplies for sculpture—Arkin thought maybe the man is having a nervous breakdown. He did not believe it. One day they met by chance in the men's room and Rubin strode out without a word. Arkin, incensed, felt for the sculptor surges of hatred. He didn't like people who didn't like him. Here I make a sociable, innocent remark to the son-of-a-bitch—at worst it might be called innocuous—and to him it's an insult. I know the type, I'll give him tit for tat. Two can play.

But when he had calmed down and was reasonable, Arkin continued to wonder and worry over what might have gone wrong. I've always thought I was good in human relationships. He had a worrisome nature and wore a thought ragged if in it lurked a fear the fault was his own. Arkin searched the past. He had always liked the sculptor even though Rubin offered only his fingertip in friendship; yet Arkin had been friendly to him—courteous, interested in his work, and respectful of his dignity, almost visibly weighted with unspoken thoughts. Had it, he often wondered, something to do with his mentioning—suggesting—not long ago, the possibility of a new exhibition of his sculpture, to which Rubin had reacted as though his life were threatened?

It was then he recalled he had never told Rubin how he had responded to his hacked driftwood show—never once commented on it although he had signed the guest book and the sculptor surely knew he had been there. Arkin hadn't liked the show yet had wanted to seek Rubin out to name one or two interesting pieces. But when he had located him in the storage room, intently involved with a folio of prints, lost in hangdog introspection so deeply he had been unwilling, or unable, to greet whoever was standing at his back—hiding, really—Arkin had said to himself, better let it be. He had ducked out of the gallery without saying a word. Nor had he mentioned the drift-wood exhibition thereafter. Was this kindness cruel? In some cases unsaid things were worse than things said. Something Rubin might think about if he hadn't.

Still it's not very likely he's avoiding me so long after the fact for that alone, Arkin reflected. If he was disap-pointed, or irritated, or both, by my not mentioning his driftwood show, he would then and there have stopped talking to me if he was going to stop talking. But he didn't. He seemed as friendly as ever, according to his measure, and he isn't a dissembler. And when I afterwards sug-gested the possibility of a new show he obviously wasn't eager to have—which touched him to torment on the spot—he wasn't at all impatient with me but only started staying out of my sight after the business of his white cap, what-ever that meant to him. Maybe it wasn't my mention of the cap itself that's annoyed him. Maybe it's a cumulative thing—three minuses for me? Arkin felt it was probably cumulative; still it seemed that the cap remark had mys-teriously wounded Rubin most, because nothing that had happened before had threatened their relationship, such as it was, and it was then at least amicable, pleasant. Having thought it through to this point Arkin had to admit to himself he did not know why Rubin acted as strangely as he was now acting.

Off and on the art historian considered going down to the basement to the sculptor's studio and there apologizing to him if he had said something inept, which he certainly hadn't meant to do. He would ask Rubin if he'd mind telling him what it was that bothered him; if it was something *else* he had inadvertently said or done, he would apologize for that and clear things up. It would be mutually beneficial. One early spring day he made up his mind to visit Rubin after his seminar that afternoon, but one of his students, a bearded printmaker, had found out it was Arkin's thirty-fifth birthday and presented the art historian with a white ten-gallon Stetson that the student's father, a traveling salesman, had brought back from Waco, Texas.

"Wear it in good health, Mr. Arkin," said the student. "Now you're one of the good guys."

Arkin was wearing the hat going up the stairs to his office, accompanied by the student who had given it to him, when they encountered the sculptor, who grimaced, then glowered in disgust. Arkin was upset, though he felt at once that the force of this uncalled-for reaction indicated that, indeed, the hat remark had been taken by Rubin as an insult. After the bearded student left Arkin he placed the Stetson on his worktable, it had seemed to him, before going to the men's room; and when he returned the cowboy hat was gone. The art historian frantically searched for it in his office and even hurried to his seminar room to see whether it could possibly have landed up there, someone having snatched it as a joke. It was not in the seminar room. Smoldering in resentment, Arkin thought of rushing down and confronting Rubin nose to nose in his studio, but could not bear the thought. What if he hadn't taken it?

Now both of them evaded the other; but after a period of rarely meeting, they began, ironically, Arkin thought, to encounter one another everywhere—even in the streets of various neighborhoods, especially near galleries on Madison, or Fifty-seventh, or in Soho; or on entering or leaving movie houses, and on occasion about to go into stores near the art school; each then hastily crossed the street to skirt the other, twice ending up standing close by on the sidewalk. In the art school both refused to serve together on committees. One, if he entered the the lavatory and saw the other, stepped outside and remained a distance away till he had left. Each hurried to be first into the basement cafeteria at lunch time because when one followed the other in and observed him standing on line at the counter, or already eating at a table, alone or in the company of colleagues, invariably he left and had his meal elsewhere. Once, when they came in together they hurriedly departed together. After often losing out to Rubin, who could get to the cafeteria easily from his studio, Arkin began to eat sandwiches in his office. Each had become a greater burden to the other, Arkin felt, than he would have been if only one were doing the shunning. Each was in the other's mind to a degree and extent that bored him. When they met

unexpectedly in the building after turning a corner or opening a door, or had come face-to-face on the stairs, one
glanced at the other's head to see what, if anything,
adorned it; they then hurried by, or away in opposite direc-
tions. Arkin as a rule wore no hat unless he had a cold, then
he usually wore a black woolen knit hat all day; and
Rubin lately affected a railroad engineer's cap. The art
historian felt a growth of repugnance for the other. He
hated Rubin for hating him and beheld hatred in Rubin's
eyes.

"It's your doing," he heard himself mutter to himself
to the other. "You brought me to this, it's on your head."

After hatred came coldness. Each froze the other out
of his life; or froze him in.

One early morning, neither looking where he was going as he rushed into the building to his first class, they
bumped into each other in front of the arched art school
entrance. Angered, insulted, both started shouting. Rubin,
his face flushed, called Arkin "murderer," and the art
historian retaliated by calling the sculptor "thief." Rubin
smiled in scorn, Arkin in pity; they then fled.

Afterwards in imagination Arkin saw them choking
one another. He felt faint and had to cancel his class. His
weakness became nausea so he went home and lay in bed,
nursing a severe occipital headache. For a week he slept
badly, felt tremors in his sleep; he ate next to nothing.
"What has this bastard done to me?" he cried aloud. Later
he asked, "What I have done to myself?" I'm in this against
the will, he thought. It had occurred to him that he found

it easier to judge paintings than to judge people. A woman had said this to him once but he had denied it indignantly. Arkin answered neither question and fought off remorse. Then it went through him again that he ought to apologize, if only because if the other couldn't he could. Yet he feared an apology would cripple his craw.

Half a year later, on his thirty-sixth birthday, Arkin, thinking of his lost cowboy hat and having heard from the Fine Arts secretary that Rubin was home sitting shiva for his recently deceased mother, was drawn to the sculptor's studio—a jungle of stone and iron figures—to search for the hat. He found a discarded welder's helmet but nothing he could call a cowboy hat. Arkin spent hours in the large sky-lighted studio, minutely inspecting the sculptor's work in welded triangular iron pieces, set amid broken stone statuary he had been collecting for years—decorative garden figures placed charmingly among iron flowers seeking daylight. Flowers were what Rubin was mostly into now, on long stalks with small corollas, on short stalks with petaled blooms. Some of the flowers were mosaics of triangles fixing white stones and broken pieces of thick colored glass in jeweled forms. Rubin had in the last several years come from abstract driftwood sculptures to figurative objects— the flowers, and some uncompleted, possibly abandoned, busts of men and women colleagues, including one that vaguely resembled Rubin in a cowboy hat. He had also done a lovely sculpture of a dwarf tree. In the far corner of the studio was a place for his welding torch and gas tanks as well as arc-welding apparatus, crowded by open heavy wooden boxes of iron triangles of assorted size and thickness. The art historian slowly studied each sculpture and after a while thought he understood why talk of a new exhibition had threatened Rubin. There was perhaps one fine piece, the dwarf tree, in the whole iron jungle. Was this what he was afraid he might confess if he fully expressed himself?

Several days later, while preparing a lecture on Rembrandt's self-portraits, Arkin, examining the slides, observed that the portrait of the painter which he had remembered as the one he had seen in the Rijksmuseum in Amsterdam was probably hanging in Kenwood House in London. And neither hat the painter wore in either gallery, though both were white, was that much like Rubin's cap. This observation startled the art historian. The Amsterdam portrait was of Rembrandt in a white turban he had wound around his head; the London portrait was him in a studio cap or beret worn slightly cocked. Rubin's white thing, on the other hand, looked more like an assistant cook's cap in Sam's Diner than it did like either of Rembrandt's hats in the large oils, or in the other self-portraits Arkin showed himself on slides. What those had in common was the unillusioned honesty of his gaze. In his self-created mirror the painter beheld distance, objectivity, painted to stare out of his right eye; but the left looked out of bedrock, beyond quality. Yet the expression of each of the portraits seemed magisterially sad; or was this what life was if when Rembrandt painted he did not paint the sadness?

After studying the pictures projected on the small screen in his dark office, Arkin felt he had, in truth, made a referential error, confusing the hats. Even so, what had Rubin, who no doubt was acquainted with the self-portraits, or may have had a recent look at them—at *what* had he taken offense? Whether I was right or wrong, so what if his white cap made me think of Rembrandt's hat and I told him so? That's not throwing rocks at his head, so what bothered him? Arkin felt he ought to be able to figure it out. Therefore suppose Rubin was Arkin and Arkin Rubin— Suppose it was me in his hat: "Here I am, an aging sculptor with only one show, which I never had confidence in and nobody saw. And standing close by, making critical pronouncements one way or another, is this art historian Arkin, a big-nosed, gawky, overcurious gent, friendly but no friend of mine because he doesn't know how to be. That's not his talent. An interest in art we have in common but not much more. Anyway, Arkin, maybe not because it means anything in particular—who says he knows what he means? —mentions Rembrandt's hat on my head and wishes me good luck in my work. So say he meant well—it's still more than I can take. In plain words it irritates me. The mention of Rembrandt, considering the quality of my work and what I am feeling generally about life, is a fat burden on my soul because it makes me ask myself once more—but once too often—why am I going on this way if this is the kind of sculptor I am going to be for the rest of my life. And since Arkin makes me think the same unhappy thing no matter what he says—or even what he doesn't say, as for instance about my driftwood show—who wants to hear more? From then on I avoid the guy—like forever."

Afterwards, after staring at himself in the mirror in the men's room, Arkin wandered on every floor of the building and then wandered down to Rubin's studio. He knocked on the door. No one answered. After a moment he tested the knob; it gave, he thrust his head into the room and called Rubin's name. Night lay on the skylight. The studio was lit with many dusty bulbs but Rubin was not present. The forest of sculptures was. Arkin went among the iron flowers and broken stone garden pieces to see if he had been wrong in his judgment. After a while he felt he hadn't been.

He was staring at the dwarf tree when the door opened and Rubin, wearing his railroad engineer's cap, in astonishment entered.

"It's a beautiful sculpture," Arkin got out, "the best in the room I'd say."

Rubin stared at him in flushed anger, his face lean; he had grown long reddish sideburns. His eyes were for once green rather than gray. His mouth worked nervously but he said nothing.

"Excuse me, Rubin, I came in to tell you I got those hats I mentioned to you some time ago mixed up."

"Damn right you did."

"Also for letting things get out of hand for a while."

"Damn right."

Rubin, though he tried not to, then began to cry. He wept silently, his shoulders shaking, tears seeping through his coarse fingers on his face. Arkin had taken off.

They stopped avoiding each other and spoke pleasantly when they met, which wasn't often. One day Arkin, when he went into the men's room, saw Rubin regarding himself in the mirror in his white cap, the one that seemed to resemble Rembrandt's hat. He wore it like a crown of failure and hope.

Notes from a Lady
at a Dinner Party

—

M A X Adler, passing through the city in November, had telephoned his old professor of architecture, Clem Harris, and was at once cordially invited to dinner that night at his house in Hempstead to meet some good friends and his young wife Karla.

She spoke of her husband's respect for Adler. "He says about you something he doesn't often say about his former students—that you deserve your success. Didn't you win an A.I.A. national medal about two years out of graduate school?"

"Not a medal," Adler explained, pleased. "It was an Honor Award certificate for a house I designed."

Adler, at the time of the dinner party, was a loose-fleshed heavy man who dressed with conservative carelessness and weighed 210.

"That's what I mean." She laughed in embarrassment and he imagined that she often laughed in embarrassment. She was strong-bodied and plain, in an elegant way, and wore her brown hair pulled back in a twist. He thought she was twenty-five or -six. She had on a short green dress with sandals, and her sturdy legs and thighs were well formed. Adler, when she asked, said he was thirty-two, and Karla remarked it was a fine age for a man. He knew her husband's age was twice his. She was direct and witty, with a certain tensity of expression, and she told him almost at once that friendship meant a lot to her.

It was during dinner that Karla Harris let Adler know about the note in his pocket. They were six at the table in the large wood-paneled dining room, with a bay window containing a pebbled bed of chrysanthemums and begonias. Besides the hosts there was a middle-aged couple, the Ralph Lewins—he was a colleague of Harris's at the Columbia University School of Architecture; and maybe to balance off Adler, Harris's secretary, Shirley Fisher, had been invited, a thin-ankled, wet-eyed divorcee in a long bright-blue skirt, who talked and drank liberally. Harris, pouring wine liberally from a bottle in a basket, sat at the head of the broad neat table, opposite Karla, who was on the qui vive to see that everything went as it should; from time to time her husband smiled his encouragement.

Max Adler sat on her right, facing Lewin across the table, and on his right was Mrs. Lewin, a small luminous-faced, listening person. Karla, when Harris was ladling turtle soup into bowls out of a handsome tureen, and the conversation was lively, leaned imperceptibly close to Adler and whispered, "If you like surprises, feel in your left pocket when you can," and though he wasn't sure at once was the proper time, when she left the room to get the rolls that had almost burned, he casually reached into his suit-coat pocket and felt a folded slip of paper which, after a minute, he smoothed out and read in his palm.

If anybody at the table had noticed that Adler's head was momentarily lowered and wondered whether he were privately saying grace, or maybe studying his wristwatch with a view to catching an early train back to the city, it occurred to him he wouldn't have worried; he was politely reading the lady's note, had initiated nothing. The slip of yellow lined paper, in small printed handwriting, said simply, "Why do we all think we *should* be happy, that it's one of the *necessary* conditions of life?" and for a while Adler, who took questions of this sort seriously, didn't know what to say in reply.

She could quite easily have asked her question while they were having cocktails on the enclosed porch and he would have done his best with it; but she had seemed concerned about the dinner and had been in and out of the kitchen many times; dealing also with the girl sitter who was putting the children to bed, really too busy to sustain a conversation with any of her guests. Yet since she hadn't orally asked her question, Adler felt he had to respect the fact that she had found it necessary to write it out on paper and slip into his pocket. If this was the way she was moved to express herself, he thought he ought to answer with a note. He glanced at her husband, aged but still vigorous since he had seen him last, who was at the moment listening attentively to Shirley. Adler excused himself—he said to get his glasses—to scribble a note on a memo pad; and when he returned, though he wasn't comfortable in pretense, he covertly passed the paper to her, grazing her warm bare thigh, though he hadn't intended to, then feeling her narrow fingers, as he touched them, close on the note.

He had been tempted to say that happiness wasn't something he worried about any more—you had it or you hadn't and why beat your brains blue when there was work to be done; but he didn't say that. He had quickly written, "Why not?—it's a short hard life if you don't outfox it."

Karla glanced at the paper in her hand, a fork in a piece of filet of sole in the other, apparently not disappointed, her color heightened, expression neutral, a bit distant. She disappeared into the kitchen with an empty salad bowl, and when she was again seated at the table, secretly passed Adler another note: "I want you to see my babies." Adler solemnly nodded as he pocketed the paper. She smiled vaguely as her husband, who had once more risen to refill the wineglasses, gazed at her fondly. The others were momentarily quietly eating, not, apparently, attentive. Karla returned a resemblance of her husband's smile as Adler, wondering why she engaged him in this curious game, felt they were now related in a way he couldn't have foreseen when he had entered the house that evening. When Harris, behind him, pouring wine into his glass, let his hand fall affectionately on his former student's shoulder, Max, who had experienced a strong emotion on seeing his old professor after so many years, felt himself resist his touch.

Later he enjoyed talking with him over brandy in the living room; it was a spacious room, twenty-four by thirty, Adler estimated, tastefully and comfortably furnished, draped, decorated, with a glass bowl of golden chrysanthemums and Shasta daisies on the fireplace mantel and some bright modernist paintings on the wall. Karla was then in the kitchen, showing the sitter how to stack and operate the dishwasher, and Adler felt geared to anticipation, though not sure of what. He tried to suppress the feeling and to some extent succeeded. But as Clem Harris poured him a cognac he stealthily felt in his pocket and there were the two notes only.

The professor, a crisp tall man with a clipped grayish beard, faintly red, and thick gray sideburns, who wore a green blazer with an orange shirt and white bow tie, was lavish in his praise of Adler's recent work, some slides of which the architect had sent him; and Max once more expressed gratitude for the interest Harris continued to show. He had always been a kind man and influential teacher.

"What are you into now?" Harris asked. After two brandies he had gone back to Scotch-and-soda. His large face was flushed and he wiped his watery eyes with a pressed handkerchief. Adler had noticed how often he glanced up at the dining-room door in anticipation of his wife's reappearance.

"The same project you saw in the transparencies," Adler said. "How about you?"

"Renovating some slum units for a private low-income housing group. There's very little money in it. It's more or less pro bono."

"I ought to be doing more of that myself."

Harris, after observing Adler for a moment, asked, "Aren't you putting on more weight, Max?"

"I eat too much," Adler confessed.

"You ought to watch your weight. Do you still smoke like a chimney?"

"Not any more."

"Bully. I wish I could get Karla to cut down."

When she reappeared his wife had brushed her hair. The green dress she had been wearing she had changed for a short crocheted strawberry mini, with white bra and half-slip showing through the weave. The warm color of the dress brought out a bloom in her face. She was an attractive woman.

"Ah, you've changed your dress," her husband said.

"I spilled at least a pint of gravy on it," Karla explained with an embarrassed laugh.

"I thought you didn't much care for this one."

"When did I say that?" she asked. "I do like it. I like it very much. It's the purple one I don't like—it's too damn harsh."

Harris, drinking from his glass, nodded pleasantly.

Something else was on his mind. "I wish you'd get yourself more help when you need it."

"What kind of help?" asked Karla.

"In the kitchen, of course." His tone was affectionate, solicitous.

"Stephanie's cleaning up—that's the dirty work."

"It was a wonderful meal," said Max.

She thanked him.

"We ought to have a maid to help at dinner parties," Harris insisted. "Sometimes our guests barely get a look at you. I wish you'd be less a puritan about occasional luxuries. I hate for you to be too tired to enjoy your own parties."

"I'm enjoying this."

Max nodded.

"You know what I mean," Harris said.

"Clem, I simply don't like maids around at small dinner parties."

She told Adler that Stephanie was another of Harris's students.

"The father of us all," she laughed.

"Stephanie needs the money," Harris said.

Karla then asked Adler if he liked her in her crocheted dress. He said he did.

"Is it too short?"

"No," said Max.

"I didn't say it was," said Harris.

The phone rang and when he answered, it was one of his doctoral candidates. Harris, good-humoredly wiggling his fingers at Karla, talked patiently with the doctoral candidate.

Adler and Karla were sitting on a love seat facing the flower-laden fireplace, when she whispered there was a note between the pillows. He recovered it as they were talking and slipped it into his pocket.

"I'll read it later."

But she had left the love seat as though to give him an opportunity to read what she had written. Karla plopped herself down next to Ada Lewin on the long beige sofa along the left wall, as Ralph Lewin, sipping a brandy, listened to Clem on the phone. Shirley Fisher then drifted over to talk with the visitor. She wore a low-draped white camisole with a slit midi and was openly flirtatious. When she crossed her legs a long thin thigh was exposed.

"Don't older woman interest you, Mr. Adler?" Her voice was slightly husky.

"I wouldn't call you old."

Shirley said she was charmed but then Karla returned. Harris was still patiently on the phone. Adler decided the colors he wore went well with the paintings on the walls. When Max was his student, Harris had worn gray suits with white shirts.

"Can you spare him for five minutes, Shirley?" Karla asked. "I want Mr. Adler to see the babies."

"Max," said Adler.

"Wouldn't they be sleeping now?"

"I want him to see them anyway—if he'd like to."

Max said he would.

He had managed to glance at her note: "Don't panic but I like you a lot."

"Enjoy yourselves," Shirley said, pouring herself a brandy.

"We will," Karla said.

As they were going up the stairs Adler said, "I wouldn't want to wake them up."

"They'll go right on sleeping."

She opened the door, switching on the light. Two children slept in cribs in a large nursery room with three curtained windows. At first Adler thought they were twins, but they weren't. One was a little girl with light-blond curls in a white crib, and the other was an infant boy in an orange crib. On the floor, in the corner, stood a circular canvas playpen strewn with dolls and wooden toys. A series of small-animal watercolors was framed on the walls; Karla said she had done them.

"I used to do such lovely watercolors."

Adler said they were charming.

"Not those, my watercolors from nature. I just haven't the time to paint any more."

"I know what you mean."

"You really don't," she said.

"This is Sara," Karla said, standing by the white crib. "She's two. Stevie is just eleven months. Look at those shoulders. Clem thought we ought to have them close together so they would be friends. His first wife died childless."

"I knew her," Adler said.

The boy, in undershirt and plastic diaper cover, lay on his side, sucking the corner of his blanket in his sleep. He resembled his father.

The little girl, asleep on her back in a flowered yellow nightgown, clutching a stuffed doll, looked like Karla.

"They're lovely children," Adler said.

Karla stood at the little girl's crib. "Oh, my babies," she said. "My little babies. My heart goes out to them." She lowered the side of the crib and, bending, kissed Sara, who opened her eyes, stared at her mother, and was then asleep, smiling.

Karla withdrew the doll and the child released it with a sigh. Then she covered the little boy with his blanket.

"Very nice children," Adler said.

"My lovely little babies. My babies, my babies." Her face was tender, sad, illumined.

"Do I sound hokey?"

"I wouldn't say so." Max was affected by her.

She lowered the shades, switched out the lights, quietly closed the door.

"Come see my study."

It was a light-curtained lavender room with a desk, portable sewing machine, and a circle of snapshots on the wall before her. Her father, who had sold insurance in Columbus, Ohio, was dead. There he was, fifty, standing in front of his automobile. The sad-faced mother had posed in her flower garden. A shot of Karla taken in college showed an attractive, sober girl with wire-frame glasses, dark eyes and brows, firm full lips. Her desk was cluttered with books, sheet music, shopping lists, correspondence.

She wanted to know if Adler had any children.

"No." He told her he had been married a short time and divorced long ago.

"You never remarried?"

"No."

"Clem married me when I was very young," Karla said.

"Didn't you marry him?"

"I mean I hardly knew what I was doing."

"What was he doing?"

"Marrying me when I was very young."

She raised the shade and stared into the night. A street light in the distance glowed through the wet window. "I always give dinner parties on rainy nights."

She said they ought to go down to the others but then opened the closet door and got out a large glossy photograph of a one-family dwelling project she had done in her architecture class with Harris.

Max said it showed promise. Karla smiled wryly.

"Really," he said.

"I love *your* work," she said. "I love the chances you take."

"If they work out right."

"They do, they do." She seemed to be trembling.

They embraced forcefully. She dug her body into his. They kissed wet-mouthed, then she broke with an embarrassed laugh.

"They'll be wondering."

"He's still on the phone," Max said, aroused.

"We'd better go down."

"What's Shirley to him?"

"A tight-jawed bitch."

"To him I said."

"He's sorry for her. Her fourteen-year-old kid is on LSD. He's sorry for everybody."

They kissed again, then Karla stepped out of his embrace and they went downstairs.

Harris was off the phone.

"I showed him our babies," Karla said to her husband.

"Showoff," smiled Harris.

"Lovely children," said Max.

Shirley winked at him.

I've lost the right to his friendship, the architect thought. A minute later he thought, Things change, they have to.

"Now please stay put for a few minutes," Harris said to Karla. "Catch your breath."

"First I have to pay Stephanie."

Harris went to his den and returned with a box of color transparencies of his renovation project for a slum-housing improvement group: before and after.

Max, his mind on Karla, examined the slides, holding each to the light. He said it was work well done.

Harris said he was gratified that Max approved.

Karla was paying Stephanie in the kitchen. Ralph Lewin, smoking a cigar, also looked at the slides, although he said he was the one who had originally taken them. Ada and Shirley were on the green sofa on the right side of the room, Ada seriously listening as Shirley went on about her son on LSD.

Karla carried in a silver trayful of bone-china cups and saucers.

"I'm always late with coffee," she remarked.

"Make mine tea," said Ralph.

She said she would get the tea in a minute.

As she handed out the coffee cups she slipped Adler a note with his.

He read it in the bathroom. "Pretend you're going to the bathroom, then go left in the back hall and you'll come out in the kitchen."

He went to the left in the hall and came out in the kitchen.

They kissed with passion.

"Where can we meet?"

"When?" Max asked.

"Tonight, maybe? I'm not sure."

"Is there a motel around?"

"Two blocks away."

"I'll get a room if you can make it. If not tonight, I could stay on till tomorrow noon. I've got to be in Boston by evening."

"I think I can. Clem and I are in separate bedrooms right now. He sleeps like dead. I'll let you know before you leave."

"Just give me a sign," Max said. "Don't write any notes."

"Don't you like them?" Karla asked.

"I do but they're risky. What if he sees you passing me one?"

"It might do him good."

"I don't want any part of that," Max said.

"I like to write notes," said Karla. "I like to write to people I like. I like to write things that suddenly occur to me. My diary was full of exciting thoughts when I was young."

"All I'm saying is it could be dangerous. Just give me a sign or say something before I leave and I'll wait till you come."

"I burned my diary last summer but I still write notes. I've always written notes to people. You have to let me be who I am."

He asked her why she had burned her diary.

"I had to. It beat me up badly." She burst into tears.

Adler left the kitchen and returned to the bathroom. He flushed the toilet, washed his hands, and reappeared in the living room. At the same moment, Karla, her face composed, brought in Ralph's tea.

For a while they talked politics across the room. Then the talk went to music and Harris put on a new recording he had bought of Mahler's "Songs of a Wayfarer." Despite the singing, Shirley talked earnestly to Ralph Lewin, who suppressed a yawn now and then. Ada and Karla were chatting about the Lewins' new house they were about to build in the spring, and Harris and Adler, on the long beige couch, discussed developments in architecture. "I might as well turn off the music," Harris said. After he had put the record away he returned and, resuming their conversation, characterized Adler's latest work as his most daring.

"That's a quality you inspired me to."

"In moderation."

Adler said he appreciated his mentor's sentiments. He felt for the first time he did not know what to say to him and it made him uncomfortable. He was now not sure whether to urge Karla to try to get out of the house tonight. On the one hand he had gratitude and loyalty to Harris to contend with; on the other he felt as though he were in love with her.

They managed to meet alone at the fireplace, when to his strange surprise she whispered, "Something's coming your way," and surreptitiously touched his hand with a folded slip of paper. Turning away from the company, Adler managed to read it, then thrust it into his pants pocket.

Karla's note said: "Can someone love someone she doesn't know?"

"We do it all the time."

"Partly I think I love you because I love your work."

"Don't confuse me with my work," Adler said. "It would be a mistake."

"It's on for tonight," she whispered.

As they stood side by side with their backs to the fireplace they reached behind them and squeezed hands.

Karla, glancing across the room at her husband, excused herself to go up to see if the babies were covered. Adler, after she had gone, tried to think of a reason to follow her upstairs, but the impulse was insane. It was past eleven and he felt nervously expectant.

When Karla came down from the nursery he heard her say to her husband, "Clem, I'm having some anxiety."

"Take a pill," Harris advised.

Adler then seriously wondered whether to tell her to
cool it for tonight. It might be better to call her from the
motel in the morning, when Harris was gone, and if she still
felt she could they would meet then. But he doubted, if
they didn't get together tonight, that she could make it in
the morning. So he decided to urge her to come as soon as
she was sure her husband was asleep.

She wants someone young for a change, he thought
It will be good for her.

Wanting to tell her the anxiety would go once they
were in bed together, Max sat down beside her on the
green sofa where she was listening distantly to Shirley
saying the drug situation had made her frantic. He waited
impatiently for one or the other to get up so that he could
say what he had to to Karla. Harris, standing nearby, con-
versing with Ada, seemed to be listening to Shirley. Karla
pretended to be unaware of Adler by her side; but after
a minute he felt her hand groping for his pocket. Without
wanting to he moved away.

Adler, just then, expected his pocket to burst into
flame. She'll write them forever, he thought; that's her
nature. If not to me, then to the next one who comes into
the house who's done something she wishes she had. He
made up his mind to return the note unread. At the same
time, with a dismaying sense of sudden loss, Adler realized
he couldn't read it if he wanted to because the paper
hadn't gone into his pocket but had fallen to the floor. The
sight of the folded yellow paper at his feet sickened the
architect. Karla was staring at it as though reliving a

dream. She had written it upstairs in her study and it said, "Darling, I can't meet you, I am six months' pregnant."

Before either of them could move to retrieve the paper, or even let it lie where it had fallen, Shirley had plucked it up.

"Did you drop this?" she asked Clem Harris.

Adler's head was thick with blood. He felt childlike and foolish. I'm disgraced and deserve it.

But Harris did not unfold the paper. He handed it to his former student. "It isn't mine, is it yours?"

"An address I wrote down," Adler said. He rose. "I have this early train to Boston to catch in the morning."

Ada and Ralph Lewin were the first to say good night.

"Bon voyage," said Shirley.

Harris brought Adler's coat and helped him on with it. They shook hands cordially.

"The air shuttle is the fastest way to Boston."

Max said he thought that was how he would go. He then said goodbye to Karla. "Thanks for having me."

"Love, marriage, happiness," Karla sang, standing in her crocheted short mini on the stairs.

She runs up to her babies in the nursery.

My Son
the Murderer

H E wakes feeling his father is in the hallway, listening. He listens to him sleep and dream. Listening to him get up and fumble for his pants. He won't put on his shoes. To him not going to the kitchen to eat. Staring with shut eyes in the mirror. Sitting an hour on the toilet. Flipping the pages of a book he can't read. To his anguish, loneliness. The father stands in the hall. The son hears him listen.

My son the stranger, he won't tell me anything.

I open the door and see my father in the hall. Why are you standing there, why don't you go to work?

On account of I took my vacation in the winter instead of the summer like I usually do.

What the hell for if you spend it in this dark smelly hallway, watching my every move? Guessing what you can't see. Why are you always spying on me?

My father goes to the bedroom and after a while sneaks out in the hallway again, listening.

I hear him sometimes in his room but he don't talk to me and I don't know what's what. It's a terrible feeling for a father. Maybe someday he will write me a letter, My dear father . . .

My dear son Harry, open up your door. My son the prisoner.

My wife leaves in the morning to stay with my married daughter, who is expecting her fourth child. The mother cooks and cleans for her and takes care of the three children. My daughter is having a bad pregnancy, with high blood pressure, and lays in bed most of the time. This is what the doctor advised her. My wife is gone all day. She worries something is wrong with Harry. Since he graduated college last summer he is alone, nervous, in his own thoughts. If you talk to him, half the time he yells if he answers you. He reads the papers, smokes, he stays in his room. Or once in a while he goes for a walk in the street.

How was the walk, Harry?

A walk.

My wife advised him to go look for work, and a couple of times he went, but when he got some kind of an offer he didn't take the job.

It's not that I don't want to work. It's that I feel bad.

So why do you feel bad?

I feel what I feel. I feel what is.

Is it your health, sonny? Maybe you ought to go to a doctor?

I asked you not to call me by that name any more. It's not my health. Whatever it is I don't want to talk about it. The work wasn't the kind I want.

So take something temporary in the meantime, my wife said to him.

He starts to yell. Everything's temporary. Why should I add more to what's temporary? My gut feels temporary. The goddamn world is temporary. On top of that I don't want temporary work. I want the opposite of temporary, but where is it? Where do you find it?

My father listens in the kitchen.

My temporary son.

She says I'll feel better if I work. I say I won't. I'm twenty-two since December, a college graduate, and you know where you can stick that. At night I watch the news programs. I watch the war from day to day. It's a big burning war on a small screen. It rains bombs and the flames go higher. Sometimes I lean over and touch the war with the flat of my hand. I wait for my hand to die.

My son with the dead hand.

I expect to be drafted any day but it doesn't bother

me the way it used to. I won't go. I'll go to Canada or somewhere I can go.

The way he is frightens my wife and she is glad to go to my daughter's house early in the morning to take care of the three children. I stay with him in the house but he don't talk to me.

You ought to call up Harry and talk to him, my wife says to my daughter.

I will sometime but don't forget there's nine years' difference between our ages. I think he thinks of me as another mother around and one is enough. I used to like him when he was a little boy but now it's hard to deal with a person who won't reciprocate to you.

She's got high blood pressure. I think she's afraid to call.

I took two weeks off from my work. I'm a clerk at the stamps window in the post office. I told the superintendent I wasn't feeling so good, which is no lie, and he said I should take sick leave. I said I wasn't that sick, I only needed a litttle vacation. But I told my friend Moe Berkman I was staying out because Harry has me worried.

I understand what you mean, Leo. I got my own worries and anxieties about my kids. If you got two girls growing up you got hostages to fortune. Still in all we got to live. Why don't you come to poker on this Friday night? We got a nice game going. Don't deprive yourself of a good form of relaxation.

I'll see how I feel by Friday, how everything is coming along. I can't promise you.

Try to come. These things, if you give them time, all

pass away. If it looks better to you, come on over. Even if it don't look so good, come on over anyway because it might relieve your tension and worry that you're under. It's not so good for your heart at your age if you carry that much worry around.

It's the worst kind of worry. If I worry about myself I know what the worry is. What I mean, there's no mystery. I can say to myself, Leo you're a big fool, stop worrying about nothing—over what, a few bucks? Over my health that has always stood up pretty good although I have my ups and downs? Over that I'm now close to sixty and not getting any younger? Everybody that don't die by age fifty-nine gets to be sixty. You can't beat time when it runs along with you. But if the worry is about somebody else, that's the worst kind. That's the real worry because if he won't tell you, you can't get inside of the other person and find out why. You don't know where's the switch to turn off. All you do is worry more.

So I wait out in the hall.

Harry, don't worry so much about the war.

Please don't tell me what to worry about or what not to worry about.

Harry, your father loves you. When you were a little boy, every night when I came home you used to run to me. I picked you up and lifted you up to the ceiling. You liked to touch it with your small hand.

I don't want to hear about that any more. It's the very thing I don't want to hear. I don't want to hear about when I was a child.

Harry, we live like strangers. All I'm saying is I remember better days. I remember when we weren't afraid to show we loved each other.

He says nothing.

Let me cook you an egg.

An egg is the last thing in the world I want.

So what do you want?

He put his coat on. He pulled his hat off the clothes tree and went down into the street.

Harry walked along Ocean Parkway in his long over-coat and creased brown hat. His father was following him and it filled him with rage.

He walked at a fast pace up the broad avenue. In the old days there was a bridle path at the side of the walk where the concrete bicycle path was now. And there were fewer trees, their black branches cutting the sunless sky. At the corner of Avenue X, just about where you can smell Coney Island, he crossed the street and began to walk home. He pretended not to see his father cross over, though he was infuriated. The father crossed over and fol-lowed his son home. When he got to the house he figured Harry was upstairs already. He was in his room with the door shut. Whatever he did in his room he was already do-ing.

Leo took out his small key and opened the mailbox. There were three letters. He looked to see if one of them was, by any chance, from his son to him. My dear father, let me explain myself. The reason I act as I do . . . There was no such letter. One of the letters was from the Post Office Clerks Benevolent Society, which he slipped into his coat pocket. The other two letters were for Harry. One was from the draft board. He brought it up to his son's room, knocked on the door and waited.

He waited for a while.

To the boy's grunt he said, There is a draft-board letter here for you. He turned the knob and entered the room. His son was lying on his bed with his eyes shut.

Leave it on the table.

Do you want me to open it for you, Harry?

No, I don't want you to open it. Leave it on the table. I know what's in it.

Did you write them another letter?

That's my goddamn business.

The father left it on the table.

The other letter to his son he took into the kitchen, shut the door, and boiled up some water in a pot. He thought he would read it quickly and seal it carefully with a little paste, then go downstairs and put it back in the mailbox. His wife would take it out with her key when she returned from their daughter's house and bring it up to Harry.

The father read the letter. It was a short letter from a girl. The girl said Harry had borrowed two of her books more than six months ago and since she valued them highly she would like him to send them back to her. Could he do that as soon as possible so that she wouldn't have to write again?

As Leo was reading the girl's letter Harry came into the kitchen and when he saw the surprised and guilty look on his father's face, he tore the letter out of his hands.

I ought to murder you the way you spy on me.

Leo turned away, looking out of the small kitchen window into the dark apartment-house courtyard. His face burned, he felt sick.

Harry read the letter at a glance and tore it up. He then tore up the envelope marked personal.

If you do this again don't be surprised if I kill you. I'm sick of you spying on me.

Harry, you are talking to your father.

He left the house.

Leo went into his room and looked around. He looked in the dresser drawers and found nothing unusual. On the desk by the window was a paper Harry had written on. It said: Dear Edith, why don't you go fuck yourself? If you write me another letter I'll murder you.

The father got his hat and coat and left the house. He ran slowly for a while, running then walking, until he saw Harry on the other side of the street. He followed him, half a block behind.

He followed Harry to Coney Island Avenue and was in time to see him board a trolleybus going to the Island. Leo had to wait for the next one. He thought of taking a taxi and following the trolleybus, but no taxi came by. The next bus came by fifteen minutes later and he took it all the way to the Island. It was February and Coney Island was wet, cold, and deserted. There were few cars on Surf Avenue and few people on the streets. It felt like snow. Leo walked on the boardwalk amid snow flurries, looking for his son. The gray sunless beaches were empty. The hot-dog stands, shooting galleries, and bathhouses were shuttered up. The gunmetal ocean, moving like melted lead, looked freezing. A wind blew in off the water and worked its way into his clothes so that he shivered as he walked. The wind white-capped the leaden waves and the slow surf broke on the empty beaches with a quiet roar.

He walked in the blow almost to Sea Gate, searching for his son, and then walked back again. On his way toward Brighton Beach he saw a man on the shore standing in the foaming surf. Leo hurried down the boardwalk stairs and onto the ribbed-sand beach. The man on the roaring shore was Harry, standing in water to the tops of his shoes.

Leo ran to his son. Harry, it was a mistake, excuse me, I'm sorry I opened your letter.

Harry did not move. He stood in the water, his eyes on the swelling leaden waves.

Harry, I'm frightened. Tell me what's the matter. My son, have mercy on me.

I'm frightened of the world, Harry thought. It fills me with fright.

He said nothing.

A blast of wind lifted his father's hat and carried it away over the beach. It looked as though it were going to be blown into the surf, but then the wind blew it toward the boardwalk, rolling like a wheel along the wet sand. Leo chased after his hat. He chased it one way, then another, then toward the water. The wind blew the hat against his legs and he caught it. By now he was crying. Breathless, he wiped his eyes with icy fingers and returned to his son at the edge of the water.

He is a lonely man. This is the type he is. He will always be lonely.

My son who made himself into a lonely man.

Harry, what can I say to you? All I can say to you is who says life is easy? Since when? It wasn't for me and it isn't for you. It's life, that's the way it is—what more can I say? But if a person don't want to live what can he do if he's dead? Nothing. Nothing is nothing, it's better to live.

Come home, Harry, he said. It's cold here. You'll catch a cold with your feet in the water.

Harry stood motionless in the water and after a while his father left. As he was leaving, the wind plucked his hat off his head and sent it rolling along the shore.

My father listens in the hallway. He follows me in the street. We meet at the edge of the water.

He runs after his hat.

My son stands with his feet in the ocean.

Talking Horse

___

Q. Am I a man in a horse or a horse that talks like a man? Suppose they took an X-ray, what would they see?—a man's luminous skeleton prostrate inside a horse, or just a horse with a complicated voice box? If the first, then Jonah had it better in the whale—more room all around; also he knew who he was and how he had got there. About myself I have to make guesses. Anyway after three days and nights the big fish stopped at Nineveh and Jonah took his valise and got off. But not Abramowitz, still on board, or at hand, after years; he's no prophet. On the contrary, he works in a sideshow full of freaks—though recently advanced, on Goldberg's insistence, to the center ring inside the big tent in an act with his deaf-mute master—Goldberg himself, may the Almighty forgive him. All I know is I've been here for years and still don't understand the nature of my fate; in short if I'm Abramowitz, a horse; or a horse *including* Abramowitz. Why is anybody's guess. Understanding goes so far and not further, especially if Goldberg blocks the way. It might be because of something I said, or thought, or did, or didn't do in my life. It's easy to make mistakes and it's easy not to know who made them. I have my theories, glimmers, guesses, but can't prove a thing.

When Abramowitz stands in his stall, his hoofs nervously booming on the battered wooden boards as he chews in his bag of hard yellow oats, sometimes he has thoughts, far-off remembrances they seem to be, of young horses racing, playing, nipping at each other's flanks in green fields; and other disquieting images that might be memories; so who's to say what's really the truth?

I've tried asking Goldberg but save yourself the trouble. He goes black-and-blue in the face at questions, really uptight. I can understand—he's a deaf-mute from way back; he doesn't like interference with his thoughts or plans, or the way he lives, and no surprises except those he invents. In other words questions disturb him. Ask him a question and he's off his usual track. He talks to me only when he feels like it, which isn't so often—his little patience wears thin. Lately his mood is awful, he reaches too often for his bamboo cane—whoosh across the rump! There's usually plenty of oats and straw and water, and once in a while even a joke to relax me when I'm tensed up, but otherwise it's one threat or another, followed by a flash of pain if I don't get something or other right, or something I say hits him on his nerves. It's not only that cane that slashes like a whip; his threats have the same effect—like a zing-zong of lightning through the flesh; in fact the blow hurts less than the threat—the blow's momentary, the threat you worry about. But the true pain, at least to me, is when you don't know what you have to know.

Which doesn't mean we don't communicate to each other. Goldberg taps out Morse code messages on my head with his big knuckle—crack crack crack; I feel the vibrations run through my bones to the tip of my tail—when he orders me what to do next or he threatens how many lashes for the last offense. His first message, I remember, was NO QUESTIONS. UNDERSTOOD? I shook my head yes and a little bell jangled on a strap under the forelock. That was the first I knew it was there.

TALK, he knocked on my head after he told me about the act. "You're a talking horse."

"Yes, master." What else can you say?

My voice surprised me when it came out high through the tunnel of a horse's neck. I can't exactly remember the occasion—go remember beginnings. My memory I have to fight to get an early remembrance out of. Don't ask me why unless I happened to fall and hurt my head or was otherwise stunted. Goldberg is my deaf-mute owner; he reads my lips. Once when he was drunk and looking for a little company he tapped me that I used to carry goods on my back to fairs and markets in the old days before we joined the circus.

I used to think I was born here.

"On a rainy, snowy, crappy night," Goldberg Morse-coded me on my skull.

"What happened then?"

He stopped talking altogether. I should know better but don't.

I try to remember what night we're talking about and certain hazy thoughts flicker in my mind, which could be some sort of story I dream up when I have nothing to do but chew oats. It's easier than remembering. The one that comes to me most is about two men, or horses, or men on horses, though which was me I can't say. Anyway two strangers meet, somebody asks the other a question and the next thing they're locked in battle, either hacking at one another's head with swords, or braying wildly as they tear flesh with their teeth; or both at the same time. If riders, or horses, one is thin and poetic, the other a fat stranger wearing a huge black crown. They meet in a stone pit on a rainy, snowy, crappy night, one wearing his cracked metal crown that weighs like a ton on his head and makes his movements slow though nonetheless accurate, and the other on his head wears a ragged colored cap; all night they wrestle by weird light in the slippery stone pit.

Q. "What's to be done?"

A. "None of those accursed bloody questions."

The next morning one of us wakes with a terrible pain which feels like a wound in the neck but also a headache. He remembers a blow he can't swear to and a strange dialogue where the answers come first and the questions follow:

I descended from a ladder.

How did you get here?

The up and the down.

Which ladder?

Abramowitz, in his dream story, suspects Goldberg walloped him over the head and stuffed him into his horse because he needed a talking one for his act and there was no such thing.

I wish I knew for sure.

DON'T DARE ASK.

That's his nature; he's a lout though not without a little consideration when he's depressed and tippling his bottle. That's when he taps me out a teasing anecdote or two. He has no visible friends. Family neither of us talks about. When he laughs he cries.

It must frustrate the owner that all he can say aloud is four-letter words like geee, gooo, gaaa, gaaw; and the circus manager who doubles as ringmaster, in for a snifter, looks embarrassed at the floor. At those who don't know the Morse code Goldberg grimaces, glares, and grinds his teeth. He has his mysteries. He keeps a mildewed three-prong spear hanging on the wall over a stuffed pony's head. Sometimes he goes down the cellar with an old candle and comes up with a new one though we have electric lights. Although he doesn't complain about his life, he worries and cracks his knuckles. Maybe he's a widower, who knows? He doesn't seem interested in women but sees to it that Abramowitz gets his chance at a mare in heat, if available. Abramowitz engages to satisfy his physical nature, a fact is a fact, otherwise it's no big deal; the mare has no interest in a talking courtship. Furthermore Goldberg applauds when Abramowitz mounts her, which is humiliating.

And when they're in their winter quarters the owner once a week or so dresses up and goes out on the town. When he puts on his broadcloth suit, diamond stickpin, and yellow gloves, he preens before the full-length mirror. He pretends to fence, jabs the bamboo cane at the figure in the glass, twirls it around one finger. Where he goes when he goes he doesn't inform Abramowitz. But when he returns he's usually melancholic, sometimes anguished, didn't have much of a good time; and in this mood may hand out a few loving lashes with that bastard cane. Or worse—make threats. Nothing serious but who needs it? Usually he prefers to stay home and watch television. He is fascinated by astronomy, and when they have those programs on the educational channel he's there night after night, staring at pictures of stars, quasars, infinite space. He also likes to read the *Daily News*, which he tears up when he's done. Sometimes he reads this book he hides on a shelf in the closet under some old hats. If the book doesn't make him laugh outright it makes him cry. When he gets excited over something he's reading in his fat book, his eyes roll, his mouth gets wet, and he tries to talk through his thick tongue, though all Abramowitz hears is geee, gooo, gaaa, gaaw. Always these words, whatever they mean, and sometimes gool goon geek gonk, in various combinations, usually gool with gonk, which Abramowitz thinks means Goldberg. And in such states he has been known to kick Abramowitz in the belly with his heavy boot. Ooof.

When he laughs he sounds like a horse, or maybe it's the way I hear him with these ears. And though he laughs once in a while, it doesn't make my life easier, because of my condition. I mean I think here I am in this horse. This is my theory though I have my doubts. Otherwise, Goldberg is a small stocky figure with a thick neck, heavy black brows, each like a small mustache, and big feet that swell up in his shapeless boots. He washes his feet in the kitchen sink and hangs up his yellowed white socks to dry on the whitewashed walls of my stall. Phoo.

He likes to do card tricks.

In winter they live in the South in a small, messy, one-floor house with a horse's stall attached that Goldberg can approach, down a few steps, from the kitchen of the house. To get Abramowitz into the stall he is led up a plank from the outside and the door shuts on his rear end. To keep him from wandering all over the house there's a slatted gate to just under his head. Furthermore the stall is next to the toilet and the broken water closet runs all night. It's a boring life with a deaf-mute except when Goldberg changes the act a little. Abramowitz enjoys it when they rehearse a new routine, although Goldberg hardly ever alters the lines, only the order of answer and question. That's better than nothing. Sometimes when Abramowitz gets tired of talking to himself, asking unanswered questions, he complains, shouts, calls the owner dirty names. He snorts, brays, whinnies shrilly. In his frustration he rears, rocks, gallops in his stall; but what good is a gallop if there's no place to go, and Goldberg can't, or won't, hear complaints, pleas, protest?

Q. "Answer me this: If it's a sentence I'm serving, how long?"

A.

Once in a while Goldberg seems to sense somebody else's needs and is momentarily considerate of Abramowitz —combs and curries him, even rubs his bushy head against the horse's. He also shows interest in his diet and whether his bowel movements are regular and sufficient; but if Abramowitz gets sentimentally careless when the owner is close by and forms a question he can see on his lips, Goldberg punches him on the nose. Or threatens to. It doesn't hurt any the less.

All I know is he's a former vaudeville comic and acrobat. He did a solo act telling jokes with the help of a blind assistant before he went sad. That's about all he's ever tapped to me about himself. When I forgot myself and asked what happened then, he punched me in the nose.

Only once, when he was half drunk and giving me my

bucket of water, I sneaked in a fast one which he answered before he knew it.

"Where did you get me, master? Did you buy me from somebody else? Maybe in some kind of auction?"

I FOUND YOU IN A CABBAGE PATCH.

Once he tapped my skull: "In the beginning was the word."

"Which word was that?"

Bong on the nose.

NO MORE QUESTIONS.

"Watch out for the wound on my head or whatever it is."

"Keep your trap shut or you'll lose your teeth."

Goldberg should read that story I once heard on his transistor radio, I thought to myself. It's about a poor cab driver driving his sledge in the Russian snow. His son, a fine promising lad, got sick with pneumonia and died, and the poor cabby can't find anybody to talk to so as to relieve his grief. Nobody wants to listen to his troubles, because that's the way it is in the world. When he opens his mouth to say a word, the customers insult him. So he finally tells the story to his bony nag in the stable, and the horse, munching oats, listens as the weeping old man tells him about his boy that he has just buried.

Something like that could happen to you, Goldberg, and you'd be a lot kinder to whoever I am.

"Will you ever free me out of here, master?"

I'LL FLAY YOU ALIVE, YOU BASTARD HORSE.

We have this act we do together. Goldberg calls it

"Ask Me Another," an ironic title where I am concerned.

In the sideshow days people used to stand among the bearded ladies, the blobby fat men, Joey the snake boy, and other freaks, laughing beyond belief at Abramowitz talking. He remembers one man staring into his mouth to see who's hiding there. Homunculus? Others suggested it was a ventriloquist's act even though the horse told them Goldberg was a deaf-mute. But in the main tent the act got thunderous storms of applause. Reporters pleaded for permission to interview Abramowitz and he had plans to spill all, but Goldberg wouldn't allow it. "His head will swell up too big," he had the talking horse say to them. "He will never be able to wear the same size straw hat he wore last summer."

For the performance the owner dresses up in a balloony red-and-white polka-dot clown's suit with a pointed clown's hat and has borrowed a ringmaster's snaky whip, an item Abramowitz is skittish of though Goldberg says it's nothing to worry about, little more than decoration in a circus act. No animal act is without one. People like to hear the snap. He also ties an upside-down feather duster on Abramowitz's head that makes him look like a wilted unicorn. The five-piece circus band ends its brassy "Overture to William Tell"; there's a flourish of trumpets, and Goldberg cracks the whip as Abramowitz, with his loose-feathered, upside-down duster, trots once around the spot-lit ring and then stops at attention, facing clown-Goldberg, his left foreleg pawing the sawdust-covered earth. They then begin the act; Goldberg's ruddy face, as he opens his painted mouth to express himself, flushes dark red, and his melancholy eyes under black brows protrude as he painfully squeezes out the abominable sounds, his only eloquence:

"Geee gooo gaaa gaaw?"

Abramowitz's resonant, beautifully timed response is:

A. "To get to the other side."

There's a gasp from the spectators, a murmur, perhaps of puzzlement, and a moment of intense expectant silence. Then at a roll of the drums Goldberg snaps the long whip and Abramowitz translates the owner's idiocy into something that makes sense and somehow fulfills expectations; though in truth it's no more than a question following a response already given.

Q. "Why does a chicken cross the road?"

Then they laugh. And do they laugh! They pound each other in merriment. You'd think this trite riddle, this sad excuse for a joke, was the first they had heard in their lives. And they're laughing at the translated question, of course, not at the answer, which is the way Goldberg has set it up. That's his nature for you. It's the only way he works.

Abramowitz used to sink into the dumps after that, knowing what really amuses everybody is not the old-fashioned tired conundrum, but the fact it's put to them by a talking horse. That's what splits the gut.

"It's a stupid little question."

"There are no better," Goldberg said.

"You could try letting me ask one or two of my own."

YOU KNOW WHAT A GELDING IS?

I gave him no reply. Two can play at that game.

After the first applause both performers take a low bow. Abramowitz trots around the ring, his head with panache held high. And when Goldberg again cracks the pudgy whip, he moves nervously to the center of the ring and they go through the routine of the other infantile answers and questions in the same silly ass-backwards order. After each question Abramowitz runs around the ring as the spectators cheer.

A. "To hold up his pants."

Q. "Why does a fireman wear red suspenders?"

A. "Columbus."

Q. "What was the first bus to cross the Atlantic?"

A. "A newspaper."

Q. "What's black and white and red all over?"

We did a dozen like that, and when we finished up, Goldberg cracked the foolish whip, I galloped a couple more times around the ring, then we took our last bows.

Goldberg pats my steaming flank and in the ocean-roar of everyone in the tent applauding and shouting bravo, we leave the ring, running down the ramp to our quarters, Goldberg's personal wagon van and attached stall; after that we're private parties till tomorrow's show. Many customers used to come night after night to watch the performance, and they laughed at the riddles though they had known them from childhood. That's how the season goes, and nothing much has changed one way or the other except that recently Goldberg, because the manager was complaining, added a couple of silly elephant riddles to modernize the act.

A. "From playing marbles."

Q. "Why do elephants have wrinkled knees?"

A. "To pack their dirty laundry in."

Q. "Why do elephants have long trunks?"

Neither Goldberg nor I think much of the new jokes but they're the latest style. I reflect that we could do the act without jokes. All you need is a talking horse.

One day Abramowitz thought he would make up a question-response of his own—it's not that hard to do. So that night after they had finished the routine, he slipped in his new riddle.

A. "To greet his friend the chicken."

Q. "Why does a yellow duck cross the road?"

After a moment of confused silence everybody cracked up; they beat themselves silly with their fists—broken straw boaters flew all over the place; but Goldberg in unbelieving astonishment glowered murderously at the horse. His ruddy face turned black. When he cracked the whip it sounded like a river of ice breaking. Realizing in fright that he had gone too far, Abramowitz, baring his big teeth, reared up on his hind legs and took several steps forward against the will. But the spectators, thinking this was an extra flourish at the end of the act, applauded wildly. Goldberg's anger apparently eased, and lowering his whip, he pretended to laugh. Amid continuing applause he beamed at Abramowitz as if he were his only child and could do no wrong, though Abramowitz, in his heart of hearts, knew the owner was furious.

"Don't forget WHO'S WHO, you insane horse," Goldberg, his back to the audience, tapped out on Abramowitz's nose.

He made him gallop once more around the ring, mounted him in an acrobatic leap onto his bare back, and drove him madly to the exit.

Afterwards he Morse-coded with his hard knuckle on the horse's bony head that if he pulled anything like that again he would personally deliver him to the glue factory. WHERE THEY WILL MELT YOU DOWN TO SIZE. "What's left over goes into dog food cans."

"It was just a joke, master," Abramowitz explained.

"To say the answer was O.K., but not to ask the question by yourself."

Out of stored-up bitterness the talking horse replied, "I did it on account of it made me feel free."

At that Goldberg whacked him hard across the neck with his murderous cane. Abramowitz, choking, staggered but did not bleed.

"Don't, master," he gasped, "not on my old wound."

Goldberg went into slow motion, still waving the cane.

"Try it again, you tub of guts, and I'll be wearing a horsehide coat with fur collar, gool, goon, geek, gonk." Spit crackled in the corners of his mouth.

Understood.

Sometimes I think of myself as an idea, yet here I stand in this filthy stall, my hoofs sunk in my yellow balls of dreck. I feel old, disgusted with myself, smelling the odor of my bad breath as my teeth in the feedbag grind the hard oats into a foaming lump, while Goldberg smokes his panatela as he watches TV. He feeds me well enough, if oats are your dish, but hasn't had my stall cleaned for a week. It's easy to get even on a horse if that's the type you are.

So the act goes on every matinee and night, keeping Goldberg in good spirits and thousands in stitches, but Abramowitz had dreams of being out in the open. They were strange dreams—if dreams; he isn't sure what they are or come from—hidden thoughts, maybe, of freedom, or some sort of self-mockery? You let yourself conceive what can't be? Anyhow, whoever heard of a talking horse's dreams? Goldberg hasn't said he knows what's going on but Abramowitz suspects he understands more than he seems to, because when the horse, lying in his dung and soiled straw, awakens from a dangerous reverie, he hears the owner muttering in his sleep in deaf-mute talk.

Abramowitz dreams, or does something of the sort, of other lives he might live, let's say of a horse that can't talk, couldn't conceive the idea; is perfectly content to be simply a horse without problems of speech. He sees himself, for instance, pulling a wagonload of yellow apples along a rural road. There are leafy beech trees on both sides and beyond them broad green fields full of wild flowers. If he were that kind of horse, maybe he might retire to graze in such fields. More adventurously, he sees himself a racehorse in goggles, thundering along the last stretch of muddy track, slicing through a wedge of other galloping horses to win by a nose at the finish; and the jockey is definitely not Goldberg. There is no jockey; he fell off.

Or if not a racehorse, if he has to be practical about it, Abramowitz continues on as a talking horse but not in circus work any longer; and every night on the stage he recites poetry. The theater is packed and people cry out oooh and aaah, what beautiful things that horse is saying.

Sometimes he thinks of himself as altogether a free "man," someone of indeterminate appearance and characteristics, who, if he has the right education, is maybe a doctor or lawyer helping poor people. Not a bad idea for a useful life.

But even if I am dreaming or whatever it is, I hear Goldberg talking in *my* sleep. He talks something like me:

As for number one, you are first and last a talking horse, not any ordinary nag that can't talk; and believe me I have got nothing against you that you *can* talk, Abramowitz, but on account of what you say when you open your mouth and break the rules.

As for a racehorse, if you take a good look at the broken-down type you are—overweight, with big sagging belly and a thick uneven dark-brown coat that won't shine up no matter how much I comb or brush you, and four hairy, thick, bent legs, plus a pair of slight cross-eyes, you would give up that foolish idea you can be a racehorse before you do something very ridiculous.

As for reciting poetry, who wants to hear a horse recite poetry? That's for the birds.

As for the last dream, or whatever it is that's bothering you, that you can be a doctor or lawyer, you better forget it, it's not that kind of a world. A horse is a horse even if he's a talking horse; don't mix yourself up with human beings if you know what I mean. If you're a talking horse that's your fate. I warn you, don't try to be a wise guy, Abramowitz. Don't try to know everything, you might go mad. Nobody can know everything; it's not that kind of a world. Follow the rules of the game. Don't rock the boat. Don't try to make a monkey out of me; I know more than you. We got to be who we are, although this is rough on both of us. But that's the logic of the situation. It goes by certain laws even though that's a hard proposition for some to understand. The law is the law, you can't change the order. That's the way things stay put together. We are mutually related, Abramowitz, and that's all there is to it. If it makes you feel any better, I will admit to you I can't live without you and I won't let you live without me. I have my living to make and you are my talking horse I use in my act to earn my living, plus so I can take care of your needs. The true freedom, like I have always told you, though you never want to believe me, is to understand that and live with it so you don't waste your energy resisting the rules; if so you waste your life. All you are is a horse who talks, and believe me, there are very few horses that can do that; so if you are smart, Abramowitz, it should make you happy instead of always and continually dissatisfied. Don't break up the act if you know what's good for you.

As for those yellow balls of your dreck, if you will behave yourself like a gentleman and watch out what you say, tomorrow the shovelers will come and after I will hose you over personally with warm water. Believe me, there's nothing like cleanliness.

Thus he mocks me in my sleep though I have my doubts that I sleep much nowadays.

In short hops between towns and small cities the circus moves in wagon vans. The other horses pull them, but Goldberg won't let me, which again wakes disturbing ideas in my head. For longer hauls, from one big city to another, we ride in red-and-white-striped circus trains. I have a stall in a freight car with some nontalking horses with fancy braided manes and sculptured tails from the bareback riders' act. None of us are much interested in each other. If they think at all they think a talking horse is a showoff. All they do is eat and drink, piss and crap, all day. Not a single word goes back or forth among them. Nobody has a good or bad idea.

The long train rides generally give us a day off without a show, and Goldberg gets depressed and surly when we're not working the matinee or evening performance. Early in the morning of a long train-ride day he starts loving his bottle and Morse-coding me nasty remarks and threats.

"Abramowitz, you think too much, why do you bother? In the first place your thoughts come out of you and you don't know that much, so your thoughts don't either. In other words don't get too ambitious. For instance what's on your mind right now, tell me?"

"Answers and questions, master—some new ones to modernize the act."

"Feh, we don't need any new ones, the act is already too long."

He should know the questions I am really asking myself, though better not.

Once you start asking questions one leads to the next and in the end it's endless. And what if it turns out I'm always asking myself the same question in different words? I keep on wanting to know why I can't ask this coarse lout a simple question about *anything*. By now I have it figured out Goldberg is afraid of questions because a question could show he's afraid people will find out who he is. Somebody who all he does is repeat his fate. Anyway, Goldberg has some kind of past he is afraid to tell me about, though sometimes he hints. And when I mention my own past he says forget it. Concentrate on the future. What future? On the other hand, what does he think he can hide from Abramowitz, a student by nature, who spends most of his time asking himself questions Goldberg won't permit him to ask, putting one and one together, and finally making up his mind—miraculous thought—that he knows more than a horse should, even a talking horse, so therefore, given all the built-up evidence, he is positively not a horse. Not in origin anyway.

So I came once more to the conclusion that I am a man in a horse and not just a horse that happens to be able to talk. I had figured this out in my mind before; then I said, no it can't be. I feel more like a horse bodywise; on the other hand I talk, I think, I wish to ask questions. So I am what I am, which is a man in a horse, not a talking horse. Something tells me there is no such thing even though Goldberg, pointing his fat finger at me, says the opposite. He lives on his lies, it's his nature.

After long days of traveling, when they were in their new quarters one night, finding the rear door to his stall unlocked—Goldberg grew careless when depressed—acting on belief as well as impulse, Abramowitz cautiously backed out. Avoiding the front of Goldberg's wagon van he trotted across the fairgrounds on which the circus was situated. Two of the circus hands who saw him trot by, perhaps because Abramowitz greeted them, "Hello, boys, marvelous evening," did not attempt to stop him. Outside the grounds, though exhilarated to be in the open Abramowitz began to wonder if he was doing a foolish thing. He had hoped to find a wooded spot to hide in for the time being, surrounded by fields in which he could peacefully graze; but this was the industrial edge of the city, and though he clop-clopped from street to street there were no woods nearby, not even a small park.

Where can somebody who looks like a horse go by himself?

Abramowitz tried to hide in an old riding-school stable and was driven out by an irate woman. In the end they caught up with him on a station platform where he had been waiting for a train. Quite foolishly, he knew. The conductor wouldn't let him get on though Abramowitz had explained his predicament. The stationmaster then ran out and pointed a pistol at his head. He held the horse there, deaf to his blandishments, until Goldberg arrived with his bamboo cane. The owner threatened to whip

Abramowitz to the quick, and his description of the effects
was so painfully vivid that Abramowitz felt as though he
had been slashed into a bleeding pulp. A half hour later he
found himself back in his locked stall, his throbbing head
encrusted with dried horse blood. Goldberg ranted in deaf-
mute talk, but Abramowitz, who with lowered head pretended contrition, felt none. To escape from Goldberg he
must first get out of the horse he was in.

But to exit a horse as a man takes some doing.
Abramowitz planned to proceed slowly and appeal to public opinion. It might take months, possibly years, to do
what he must. Protest! Sabotage if necessary! Revolt! One
night after they had taken their bows and the applause was
subsiding, Abramowitz, raising his head as though to
whinny his appreciation of the plaudits, cried out to all
assembled in the circus tent, "Help! Get me out of here,
somebody! I am a prisoner in this horse! Free a fellow
man!"

After a silence that rose like a dense forest, Goldberg, who was standing to the side, unaware of Abramowitz's passionate cry—he picked up the news later from the
ringmaster—saw at once from everybody's surprised and
startled expression, not to mention Abramowitz's undis-
guised look of triumph, that something had gone seriously
amiss. The owner at once began to laugh heartily, as
though whatever it was that was going on was more of the
same, part of the act, a bit of personal encore by the horse.
The spectators laughed too, and again warmly applauded.

"It won't do you any good," the owner Morse-coded

Abramowitz afterwards. "Because nobody is going to believe you."

"Then please let me out of here on your own account,
master. Have some mercy."

"About that matter," Goldberg rapped out sternly, "I
am already on record. Our lives and livings are dependent
one on the other. You got nothing substantial to complain
about, Abramowitz. I'm taking care on you better than you
can take care on yourself."

"Maybe that's so, Mr. Goldberg, but what good is it
if in my heart I am a man and not a horse, not even a talking one?"

Goldberg's ruddy face blanched as he Morse-coded
the usual NO QUESTIONS.

"I'm not asking, I'm trying to tell you something very
serious."

"Watch out for hubris, Abramowitz."

That night the owner went out on the town, came
back dreadfully drunk, as though he had been lying with
his mouth open under a spigot pouring brandy; and he
threatened Abramowitz with the trident spear he kept in
his trunk when they traveled. This is a new torment.

Anyway, the act goes on but definitely altered, not
as before. Abramowitz, despite numerous warnings and
various other painful threats, daily disturbs the routine.
After Goldberg makes his idiot noises, his geee gooo gaaa
gaaw, Abramowitz purposely mixes up the responses to the
usual ridiculous riddles.

A. "To get to the other side."

Q. "Why does a fireman wear red suspenders?"

A. "From playing marbles."

Q. "Why do elephants have long trunks?"

And he adds dangerous A.'s and Q.'s without permission despite the inevitability of punishment.

A. "A talking horse."

Q. "What has four legs and wishes to be free?"

At that nobody laughed.

He also mocked Goldberg when the owner wasn't attentively reading his lips; called him "deaf-mute," "stupid ears," "lock mouth"; and whenever possible addressed the public, requesting, urging, begging their assistance.

"Gevalt! Get me out of here! I am one of you! This is slavery! I wish to be free!"

Now and then when Goldberg's back was turned, or when he was too lethargic with melancholy to be much attentive, Abramowitz clowned around and in other ways ridiculed the owner. He heehawed at his appearance, brayed at his "talk," stupidity, arrogance. Sometimes he made up little songs of freedom as he danced on his hind legs, exposing his private parts. And at times Goldberg, to mock the mocker, danced gracelessly with him—a clown with a glum-painted smile, waltzing with a horse. Those who had seen the act last season were astounded, stunned by the change, uneasy, as though the future threatened.

"Help! Help, somebody help me!" Abramowitz pleaded, but nobody moved.

Sensing the tension in and around the ring, the audience sometimes booed the performers, causing Goldberg, in his red-and-white polka-dot suit and white clown's cap, great embarrassment, though on the whole he kept his cool during the act and never used the ringmaster's whip. In fact he smiled as he was insulted, whether he "listened" or not. He heard what he saw. A sly smile was fixed on his face and his lips twitched. And though his fleshy ears flared like torches at the gibes and mockeries he endured, Goldberg laughed to the verge of tears at Abramowitz's sallies and shenanigans; many in the big tent laughed along with him. Abramowitz was furious.

Afterwards Goldberg, once he had stepped out of his clown suit, threatened him to the point of collapse, or flayed him viciously with his cane; and the next day fed him pep pills and painted his hide black before the performance so that people wouldn't see the wounds.

"You bastard horse, you'll lose us our living."

"I wish to be free."

"To be free you got to know when you are free. Considering your type, Abramowitz, you'll be free in the glue factory."

One night when Goldberg, after a day of profound depression, was listless and logy in the ring, could not evoke so much as a limp snap out of his whip, Abramowitz, thinking that where the future was concerned, glue factory or his present condition of life made little difference, determined to escape either fate; he gave a solo performance for freedom, the best of his career. Though desperate, he entertained, made up hilarious riddles: A. "By jumping through the window." Q. "How do you end the pane?"; he recited poems he had heard on Goldberg's radio, which sometimes stayed on all night after the owner had fallen asleep; he also told stories and ended the evening with a moving speech.

He told sad stories of the lot of horses, one, for instance, beaten to death by his cruel owner, his brains battered with a log because he was too weakened by hunger to pull a wagonload of wood. Another concerned a racehorse of fabulous speed, a sure winner in the Kentucky Derby, had he not in his very first race been doped by his avaricious master who had placed a fortune in bets on the next best horse. A third was about a fabulous flying horse shot down by a hunter who couldn't believe his own eyes. And then Abramowitz told a story of a youth of great promise, who, out for a stroll one spring day, came upon a goddess bathing naked in a stream. As he gazed at her beauty in amazement and longing she let out a piercing scream to the sky. The youth took off at a fast gallop, realizing from the snorting, and sound of pounding hoofs as he ran, that he was no longer a youth of great promise but a horse running.

Abramowitz then cried out to the faces that surrounded him, "I also am a man in a horse. Is there a doctor in the house?"

Dead silence.

"Maybe a magician?"

No response but nervous tittering.

He then delivered an impassioned speech on freedom for all. Abramowitz talked his brains blue, ending once more with a personal appeal. "Help me to recover my original form. It's not what I am but what I wish to be. I wish to be what I really am which is a man."

At the end of the act many people in the tent were standing wet-eyed and the band played "The Star-Spangled Banner."

Goldberg, who had been dozing in a sawdust pile for a good part of Abramowitz's solo act, roused himself in time to join the horse in a bow. Afterwards, on the enthusiastic advice of the circus manager, he changed the name of the act from "Ask Me Another" to "Goldberg's Varieties." And wept himself for unknown reasons.

Back in the stall after the failure of his most passionate, most inspired, pleas for assistance, Abramowitz butted his head in frustration against the stall gate until his nostrils bled into the feedbag. He thought he would drown in the blood and didn't much care. Goldberg found him lying on the floor in the dirty straw, half in a faint, and revived him with aromatic spirits of ammonia. He bandaged his nose and spoke to him in a fatherly fashion.

"That's how the mop flops," he Morse-coded with his blunt fingertip, "but things could be worse. Take my advice and settle for a talking horse, it's not without distinction."

"Make me either into a man or make me either into a horse," Abramowitz pleaded. "It's in your power, Goldberg."

"You got the wrong party, my friend."

"Why do you always say lies?"

"Why do you always ask questions you can't ask?"

"I ask because I am. Because I wish to be free."

"So who's free, tell me?" Goldberg mocked.

"If so," said Abramowitz, "what's to be done?"

DON'T ASK I WARNED YOU.

He warned he would punch his nose; it bled again.

Abramowitz later that day began a hunger strike which he carried on for the better part of a week; but Goldberg threatened force-feeding with thick rubber tubes in both nostrils, and that ended that. Abramowitz almost choked to death at the thought of it. The act went on as before, and the owner changed its name back to "Ask Me Another." When the season was over the circus headed south, Abramowitz trotting along in a cloud of dust with the other horses.

Anyway I got my own thoughts.

One fine autumn, after a long hard summer, Goldberg washed his big feet in the kitchen sink and hung his smelly white socks to dry on the gate of Abramowitz's stall before sitting down to watch astronomy on ETV. To see better he placed a lit candle on top of the color set. But he had carelessly left the stall gate open, and Abramowitz hopped up three steps and trotted through the messy kitchen, his eyes flaring. Confronting Goldberg staring in awe at the universe on the screen, he reared with a bray of rage, to bring his hoofs down on the owner's head. Goldberg, seeing him out of the corner of his eye, rose to protect himself. Instantly jumping up on the chair, he managed with a grunt to grab Abramowitz by both big ears as though to lift him by them, and the horse's head and neck, up to an old wound, came off in his hands. Amid the stench of blood and bowel a man's pale head popped out of the hole in the horse. He was in his early forties, with fogged pince-nez, intense dark eyes, and a black mustache. Pulling his arms free, he grabbed Goldberg around his thick neck with both bare arms and held on for dear life. As they tugged and struggled, Abramowitz, straining to the point of madness, slowly pulled himself out of the horse up to his navel. At that moment Goldberg broke his frantic grip and, though the astronomy lesson was still going on in a blaze of light, disappeared. Abramowitz later made a few discreet inquiries, but no one could say where.

Departing the circus grounds he cantered across a grassy soft field into a dark wood, a free centaur.